COME HAVE

A GO IF YOU

THINK YOU'RE

RICH

ENOUGH!

Haydn Middleton

Hippo

For Alex and Sarah – Rich? They're Royals!

3 330 485 21

Scholastic Children's Books,
Commonwealth House, 1–19 New Oxford Street,
London, WC1A 1NU, UK
a division of Scholastic Ltd
London ~ New York ~ Toronto ~ Sydney ~ Auckland
Mexico City ~ New Delhi ~ Hong Kong

First published in the UK by Scholastic Ltd, 1999

Text copyright © Haydn Middleton, 1999
Illustrations copyright © Philip Reeve, 1999

ISBN 0 439 01083 7

Typeset by DP Photosetting, Aylesbury, Bucks
Printed and bound by Bath Press, Bath

1 2 3 4 5 6 7 8 9 10

The rights of Haydn Middleton and Philip Reeve to be
identified respectively as the author and illustrator of this work have
been asserted by them in accordance with the Copyright,
Designs and Patents Act, 1988.

1

The ball dropped down in front of Gaffer Mann. He was deep inside his own half. No opposing forward was anywhere near. But the Castle Albion skipper wasn't having one of his better games. He took a wild swing, miskicked horribly – and the ball soared out of Albion's Ash Acre stadium into the street.

The ref signalled for a new ball but nothing happened. It was the third time Gaffer had hoofed a ball over the North Stand that afternoon. Kids outside had run off with the other two, and Albion were so short of funds that this was their last one. So while officials from club sponsors Lampshades Plus rushed out of the ground to get it back, all the players were left to twiddle their thumbs.

One of them was schoolboy superstar Luke Green: Albion's midfield maestro and the youngest-ever player in British football. But as he paused to catch his breath, he was feeling twice his age. It was four-thirty on Saturday,

April the twenty third – St George's Day. And as far as Luke was concerned, he was fighting a whole herd of dragons here. Dragons in green and black football kit who called themselves Chester City FC. They were *just* as fierce in the tackle as any mythical beast that old St George had faced. And with fifteen minutes left to play, they were leading Castle Albion by a goal to nil.

The ref looked impatiently at his watch. Still no sign of the ball. On three sides of the shabby old ground the 4,568 crowd was pretty well silent. Almost all the noise was coming from behind the Town End goal where Chester's two hundred travelling fans were gathered. *Almost* all the noise.

The rest came from one man on the touchline by the home dug-out. He was dressed in a huge sheepskin coat that seemed to merge with his own bushy beard. And as he roared and screamed at each Albion player in turn, he waved his arms as if he'd been in a straitjacket for ten years and had just been set free. To be honest, he looked nutty enough to be put back inside one now. But he was only doing his job – for this was Albion's manager, Mr Benny Webb.

"Tuck in more Craig...! Square on, Chrissie, square on...! Get in the hole, Carl. Get in the 'ole and stay there!"

Each player nodded. Some gave him the thumbs up. None of them really understood what he was going on about, but Benny's tactics never made much sense during games. The actual words weren't all that important. His message, however, was crystal clear: *You can't lose this one! You CAN'T!*

And they couldn't. Not if they wanted to climb off the bottom of the Nationwide League Division Three table. Already they were two points behind Shrewsbury and Exeter, the two teams just above them. And after this, there were only four League games left. Four games for Castle Albion to escape from automatic relegation to the Football Conference.

Suddenly the ball was hurled back on to the pitch. As the Chester wing-back collected it and shaped up to take the throw, Benny windmilled his arms so fast that Luke thought he might take off like a great sheepskin helicopter. "Now *concentrate*, the lot of you!" he bellowed. "And *forget* about the *Cup*!"

Forget about the Cup, thought Luke, darting over to intercept the throw-in, slipping away from his marker and glancing up to see who was making a forward run. *Forget about the Cup...* Veteran striker Ruel Bibbo was wide on the left, YTS winger Chrissie Pick was arrowing in on goal from the right, Carl Davey was heading for the penalty spot. But all three were tightly marked.

Luke took the ball on. All the free Chester

defenders were backing off. He had a clear sight of goal but it was still forty yards away. Too far. Then a blue-and-white-hooped blur raced past him towards the right-hand corner flag. It was stylish centre-back Cool Frederick Dulac, Albion's other stellar schoolboy – and Luke's best mate too.

No one was picking him up so Luke lasered the ball ten yards ahead of the Cool One, then tore upfield himself. Frederick didn't even look to check that Luke was making his run. They'd worked this move a thousand times in the park. A million. They could have done it in their sleep.

Cool F caught up with the ball, strode over it, then played a sweet reverse pass into Luke's path with the back of his heel. That caught three Chester defenders off-balance and took them out completely – leaving Luke with a free shot from the edge of the box. He hit it first time. Both barrels. The keeper barely moved as it flew low and hard inside his right-hand post.

One-one!

Now the home fans found their voices:

"Albion... Castle Albion... We'll Support You Evermore!"

rang out loud and clear – as it usually did whenever their team wasn't losing. Nine guys in blue-and-white were piling on top of the goalscorer but over by the touchline Benny Webb wanted none of that. "Get back! Get back!" he windmilled. "We wanna *win* this! Keep your eyes on *this* prize! Don't even *think* about Wembley!"

No Cup, no Wembley, Luke reminded himself as he trotted back, turned round, and watched Chester restart the game. Then he set his brilliant football brain to work on how to open up Chester City a second time. The moment came with four minutes left on the clock.

Now that Albion were level, Gaffer Mann seemed a lot less twitchy. Several times Luke laid easy balls back to him to punt upfield, and none of them went *near* the North Stand roof. Gaffer was no Frank Leboeuf but he had the heart of a lion, and Albion always seemed to have an extra man when he was on song. Now he joined the attack more and more, fearlessly putting himself about in the Chester penalty area, looking to create a match-winning chance.

From one of his knock-downs, central midfielder Michael "Half-Fat" Milkes brought a fine fingertip save from the Chester keeper. Luke sprinted over to take the corner. There was no time to lose. Every Albion player except goalie Madman Mort had come forward. Luke could see the Chester defenders desperately trying to get them all marked. But for a split second one big blue-and-white shirt got free near the penalty spot. That was all Luke needed.

He stroked across an inch-perfect out-swinging corner. The unmarked Gaffer Mann rose to meet it with a bullet header. *In* went his first goal of the season. *Up* went a mighty roar of relief and joy from the Albion faithful. *Down* went ten Albion outfield players in a heap on top of the goalscorer.

Chester attacked like men possessed in the closing minutes. But Albion clung on, and when the final whistle went they had all three points in the bag. Luke grinned and closed his eyes as the celebrations erupted around him.

Now, just for a bit, he could think about the Cup. *Now* he could dream about Wembley. Because in exactly three weeks time that was where they were all going to be: lining up for the FA Cup Final – against Manchester United!

"If you carry on at Wembley like you finished today," chirped club physio Terry Vaudeville, "you'll *thrash* That Other Lot! Beckham, Giggs, Yorke, Keane – you'll have 'em all for breakfast!"

"Suits me!" said goalie Madman, licking his lips and rubbing his outsized belly.

"Yeah, yeah," called out Trinidadian midfielder Narris Phiz, "You've never been slow to stuff yourself stupid! But have you got the *stomach* for That Other Lot? It's gonna be *rich* meat."

"Oh, the richest!" defender Dennis Meldrum agreed.

"Absolutely *prime*!" laughed fellow defender Craig Edwards. "*Premier*, even!"

Then all the players in the Albion dressing room broke into: "We're gonna win the Cup! We're gonna win the CUP!"

And even now – two weeks after they had shocked the entire football world by overcoming Arsenal in the FA Cup semi-final – you could still hear the amazement in their voices.

No team from the lowest division had ever got to the Final before – let alone one lying ninety-second in the League! But little Castle Albion had pulled it off. Saving all their best performances for the Cup, they'd got past Villa, Wolves, Newcastle and Liverpool as well as the Arsenal. And on Saturday, May the fourteenth, they were scheduled to play That Other Lot under the twin towers.

That Other Lot. No one ever said the name of Albion's Cup Final opponents. Over the past two weeks it had become an unspoken law at Ash Acre. Luke knew why. Just to think the name of that great, all-conquering club – Man U, Man U, Man U, Man U! – was enough to make you tremble. And then to think you had to *play* against them! Eleven on eleven. At Wembley! Whooooooooah!

"What's up with you, Big Man?" Terry V asked Ruel Bibbo when the chanting fizzled out. "Don't tell me you've done your groin in again?"

Everyone groaned as their eyes swivelled to the number nine. Ruel was sitting holding the top of his leg, with his face twisted in pain. "Yeah," he gasped. "I felt it go right at the end there." Everyone groaned even louder. Back in the eighties, the ex-West Brom, Chelsea and

Tottenham man had been an England international – one of the first black strikers to play for his country. Now in the twilight of his career, the spirit was still willing but the flesh was frequently weak. Especially the flesh in the region of his left groin.

"Up on the bench with you, then," sighed Terry, as Ruel limped across the dressing room towards him. "Let's take a look at the damage."

While the others began to strip off for their bath, Luke quickly pulled a sweater and jeans over his kit. He had to get home – and fast. For all his brilliance on the pitch, he had a major problem off it. His mum.

The woman loathed *everything* to do with football – right through the alphabet from Adidas to Zola. Months before, on finding out that Luke was playing for a professional team, she had thrown the mother of all wobblers. She'd told him she would skin him alive if he even *watched* another Albion game. And as far as she knew, he'd never kicked or headed a ball from that moment on.

Luckily for Luke, his dad, stepdad, grandparents and headmistress were all big footie fans. With their help, he still managed to play in most of Albion's games – but keeping his mum in the dark could be a tense business. Like now. He'd told her at two-thirty that he was going to the library to check some facts for his History homework on the six wives of Henry VIII. If he didn't get home soon, his mum would get so suspicious that *his* head might end up on the block.

But before he could say a quick goodbye and make his getaway, the door opened and in came Benny Webb. Now Benny never looked particularly happy. It was something to do with that great sheepskin coat of his. It seemed to weigh him down, as if he was carrying the whole world on his shoulders. But now Benny looked so down in the mouth, his lower lip could have been brushing his Hush Puppies. He closed the door firmly behind him.

"Hey cheer up, Boss!" cried Half-Fat Milkes. "We won – remember!"

Slowly Benny nodded his big bearded head. "Yeah, but so did Shrewsbury. And Exeter got a draw at Darlington. We're still bottom on goals scored."

"Never mind, though," Chrissie Pick put in, smoothing down The Biggest Hair In The Nationwide League after pulling off his shirt. "Still four games left. And three of 'em are at home."

Again Benny nodded. This didn't seem to console him much. "There's more bad news though, lads," he said. "I think you'd all better sit down to hear it."

Everyone – including Luke – did just that as an

odd hush fell on the dressing room. What on earth was Benny going to tell them? That the FA had decided not to let a Third Division side play at Wembley after all? That the bath was going to be cold again because the club still couldn't afford to repair the boiler? "As you know," he began, "with regard to finances, we've been struggling here for some time now..."

"'We're so poor we can hardly pay attention!'" mimicked Narris. That was one of Benny's favourite sayings.

"Spot on," said Benny solemnly. "It goes way back. Before your time. Before mine. Crazy transfer fees. Loans taken out and never paid back. Directors with their fingers in the till and fiddling the tax returns. It's a long, sad, sorry story," he paused, "and now it looks like the end's in sight."

"What d'you mean, Boss?" Terry asked, looking up from Ruel's groin.

"I mean that our sponsors have just gone bust. As of an hour ago, Lampshades Plus are – technically – Lampshades Minus. And since they were the only people keeping us afloat, we're now goin' the same way. We're seven million quid in debt. We've got eighteen days to pay it off. If we don't, it's Goodnight Albion."

Luke, like everyone else, tried to work out the date of the wind-up deadline. Cool Frederick, as quick upstairs as he was on his feet, got there first: "The Wednesday before Wembley," he almost whispered.

"That's right," said Benny. "If someone don't put their hand in their pocket and buy this club, we're gonna go out of business before the Cup Final."

Before this could sink in properly there was another knock at the door.

No one moved. No one spoke. They were all too shell-shocked. Another knock followed, a bit louder. Five more silent seconds passed.

"Hadn't you better answer that, Boss?" murmured Terry. "It might be our fairy godmother with seven million quid straight out of her Swiss bank account."

Still staring at the floor, Benny flung out a hand behind him and tore the door open. At that very moment the person outside reached forward to knock a third time – with far more force than before. Too late he saw the door whip back. His momentum carried him fist-first into the dressing room – and face-first into the side of the high wooden wall-unit with spaces for all the players' boots.

He smacked into it like a wasp hitting a window. He made a bit of a buzzing noise too as he sank to the muddy floor in his sleek Boss suit.

He even *looked* slightly waspy in his Rayban shades and mustard-coloured fake tan.

"Oh, it's you Vealy," said Benny, turning to watch him stagger back to his feet. "Come on in, why don't you?"

The new arrival gave a lopsided golden-toothed grin, then ran a hand through his heavily-gelled hair. His name was Neil Veal, Commercial Agent to the Stars – or so it said on his card – and he had two of the Albion players on his roster as well. Not the two players he *really* wanted, though. For months he'd been trying to sign up Luke and Cool F, to make some sleazy cash-ins on their new-found fame – so far without a whiff of success.

"No damage done," he leered, although no one had asked him if he was OK. "Bump on the nose. No biggie!" Only then did he glance around at all the mournful faces. "Hey, what's with you guys? Did somebody die?"

"You could say that," Benny told him. "Who are you after, anyway? If it's Chrissie and Madman, you'll have to wait till after this team meeting."

"Well as it happens," Agent Veal smoothly replied, "it's *not* just Chrissie and Madman who might be interested in this latest little deal I'm finessing..."

"Wouldn't be anything to do with Wash and Go, would it?" Chrissie snorted, giving his huge hair a pacifying pat, as if it might fly up and have a go at the agent of its own accord. "You've been promising me a telly advert for them ever since the Fourth Round."

Veal shot him a metallic smile. "This close, Chrissie," he said, holding his thumb and first finger half a centimetre apart. "On my life – it's *this* close." Then he swung his attention back to everyone else. "But listen up – I've had talks this week with a *major* recording company. They liked my pitch, and now they've agreed to let you cut your very own Cup Final Squad single..."

"*Woo-Woo-WOOO!*" went just about everyone in the room. "*Squad!*" muttered Benny, who'd bought his last single when people still had wind-up gramophones. "We've only got fourteen players on the books – and that includes the ballboys."

"*JUST AS LONG...*" Vealy continued, getting some hush again. "Just as long as we can get a real pop celebrity to record alongside us."

That took the wind out of everyone's sails. "Well haven't *you* got any pop stars on your roster?" Craig Edwards asked the agent.

"Pop stars?" Madman laughed. "Male strippers, yes. Cilla-Black-O-Grams, maybe. Pop stars? *I don't think so!*"

Veal straightened his tie, choosing to ignore that. "So I've been chasing up a few of my contacts in the biz," he went on. "Unfortunately Elton John is tied up – and besides, he's Watford. I've left a message on Sporty Spice's machine. David Baddiel was interested and might call me back, although he thought he'd probably peaked already with 'Three Lions'..."

"How about getting Take That to re-form and record with us?" sneered Carl Davey, obviously not believing a word Neil Veal was saying. "Or Abba, even?"

"And what about The Beatles?" suggested Dennis. "They could use a hit."

"Face it, Vealy," Big Ruel winced, up on the physio's bench, "we're not glamorous enough. What kind of musician's gonna want to record with us?"

"Well, there's always Luke's dad," Terry piped up. And then a far deeper hush than before descended on them all.

Luke's dad had been trying (and, frankly, failing) to hit the charts for nearly thirty years. All his music was rooted in the sixties but even back then he'd have struggled to find an audience. He didn't sing well, he didn't play guitar well, and he certainly didn't write any decent songs. Luke loved the guy to bits but there was no getting away from one fact: he was *never* going to make it – however many times he changed his name. (The latest had been from just plain Green to The Artist

Formerly Known As Green – or TAFKAG for short.)

Then a surprising voice broke the silence. "Yo, Terry. Nice call." Everyone's head swung towards Cool Frederick Dulac. Now here was a guy who *could* sing. At the club's Karaoke Fundraiser he'd brought the house down. He knew his music too – and ran a rare records search service from his own home. "Give the gig to TAFKAG," he said to Vealy, sticking a finger into his post-match bag of sherbet then sucking it. Cool F had always had a soft spot for Luke's dad. Perhaps it was just pity. "He was chillin' at my place last week with Luke. We jammed. It was cool. We could work up a track together."

The agent gulped. He'd have gulped twice if he'd *heard* that jam session. Luke had hardly been able to stay in the same room. Frederick was wicked on vocals – but his dad's lyrics! They made Steps sound like Shakespeare.

"Well, hey," said Vealy, looking almost frightened. "TAFKAG, eh? *Maybe* for now I'll just keep following up my own contacts. The session would be this Friday so I've got till then. But *possibly*, just possibly, if no one else..."

If he finished the sentence Luke didn't hear. Instead he looked at his watch, saw how late it was, and rushed off home with a flying wave at the unlikeliest bunch of recording artists he'd *ever* seen.

On Tuesday night Albion were away at Cardiff. Luke wasn't. As the game kicked off, he was stuck in his sitting room with his mum and stepdad Rodney, watching a TV programme about country mansions. Luke's mum liked a nice big house – especially if it had a nice big landscaped garden. And on this programme you couldn't move for lawns and lakes and statues and ha-has.

"What exactly *is* a ha-ha, dear?" Rodney asked timidly at one point.

"A sunken fence around a park," she snapped back, without un-gluing her eyes from the screen. For her, this was about as good as it got.

Luke stared blankly at all the grass. The grass on the pitch at Ninian Park, Cardiff, wouldn't be half as neat. By this stage of the season there would be bald patches all over it. But that, more than anywhere in the world, was where Luke wanted to be. And he *could* have been. Between them, his dad, headmistress, stepdad and grandparents could surely have got him there in time. But then his mum had suggested that the three of them should have a quiet evening in watching the programme about stately homes. And a suggestion from her was a bit like a tax demand from the Inland Revenue. You didn't *have* to take any notice of it. It all depended on how much you liked prison food.

"I'm just going to get some crisps," Luke said at the End Of Part One. His mum had done fishfingers for dinner but it must have been a one-handed fish because there'd been precious few of them and now he was starving. There was another reason, though, why he wanted to get into the kitchen.

As soon as he was out there he switched on the radio. With the volume turned down low, he tuned into the local radio station. There was always a live commentary on Albion's games, and Luke found it just as the half-time whistle went at Cardiff. Ducking closer to the speaker he held his breath and listened:

"*Well, after forty-five it's nil-nil. Injury-hit Albion are giving it their best, but with Ruel Bibbo out for at least ten days with a groin strain* (Ten Days! thought Luke, his jaw dropping) *they're woefully short of firepower up front. His surprise replacement in the Albion starting line-up, club physio Terry Vaudeville* (Terry! thought Luke, his jaw hitting the work-surface) *has made a few good runs but you have to say he doesn't look match-fit* (I should think not! thought Luke. He retired eight seasons ago!) *and you can't really see where an Albion goal is going to come from. Meanwhile at the back Frederick Dulac is marshalling the defence quite superbly, but in midfield – oh how Albion are missing that little bit extra that young Luke Green always gives them...*"

Just then Luke heard footsteps in the hall. Quick as a flash he turned the radio off, grabbed a bag of crisps from the larder, ripped it open and crammed a fistful into his mouth – realizing too late that they were a foul Pickled Onion and Gherkin flavour, and a year past their sell-by date from the taste of them.

"It's only me," whispered Rodney, coming in. He hadn't taken off the pink pinny he wore for washing up. This pinny had a history. Rod had had it on when Albion beat Villa in the Third Round live on TV. Thinking it must be a lucky charm, he'd then worn it for every other Round too. And now he'd even started wearing it during League games. "Did you get the half-time score?"

"Nil-nil," Luke whispered back as he chewed on the filthy crisps. "And you'll never guess what – Terry V's up front 'cos Ruel's out for *ten days*!"

"*Ten days! Terry!*"

It was no good. These crisps weren't fit for human consumption. Luke went to the swing-bin and spat them into it, then chucked the rest of the bag in too. It landed on a screwed-up page from that morning's *Daily Mail*. A football page. Luke's mum always ripped out the football pages before reading the rest of the paper. Which was just as well. Otherwise she'd soon have found out that her son was still appearing for the Albion. The headline on this page was about Albion too.

THE COLLAPSING CASTLE! it said, above the latest update on the club's desperate fight to stay in business – and below it was a cartoon of Ash Acre, drawn in the style of a fortress falling apart.

"Come on!" came the command from the sitting room. "It's starting again! And bring me some Pickled Onion and Gherkin crisps. I think there's one bag left."

The programme dragged on endlessly. Oh how, how, *how* were Albion doing? All Luke could imagine was poor old Terry Vaudeville huffing and puffing about in a hooped shirt. He'd been a solid enough performer in his day – Brentford, Northampton, Colchester, Southend. But what a time to have to blow the cobwebs off your boots – at Albion's last away game of this topsy-turvy season (unless you counted the Cup Final at Wembley – although *that* meant counting on Albion still being in existence on the fourteenth of May).

At nine thirty-two the phone rang. Luke's mum was nearest so she answered. "Yes, yes, we've agreed on all that," she said after a moment. "He'll come to you after school on Friday and I want him back after lunch on Sunday." Luke sat up. It was his dad, calling about the weekend arrangements. "Look, this is a *very* inconvenient time, you know. And where are you phoning from? What's all that booing in the background? Are you playing one of your gigs?"

Luke sat up straighter still. His dad wasn't gigging. He was at Ninian Park – where the game had just ended. Since the Albion couldn't afford coaches now, he took two or three players to each away game in his multi-coloured van. But who was doing the booing – the home or away fans? What had *happened*?

"Yes all right," said Luke's mum, "you can have a *quick* word with him. But we *are* trying to enjoy a TV programme here." She passed the phone across Rodney to Luke who was sitting at the end of the sofa.

"Hi, guy!" came the unmistakable sound of TAFKAG. "I know your mum's just a shot away so just keep saying 'Right' – right?"

"Right."

"It ended nil-nil." So *both* sets of fans were booing. "Exeter drew too."

"Ri-ight." Oh flip. Five times over.

"But hey, Frederick and I wrote a real groovy track coming here. It'll be *fab* for the Cup Final single! We'll unveil it at training tomorrow. Keep on truckin' now!"

"Ri-i-i-i-ght," said Luke – wondering whether to be more worried by Albion's iffy result or the thought of his drippy-hippy dad performing in the morning.

5

Luke's headmistress let him off lessons just once a week for training. Cool Frederick, who lived with his elder sister, had a far looser arrangement with the school. He more or less came and went as he pleased. But since he seemed to know more than most of his teachers, no one kicked up much of a fuss. And besides, he had his rare records business to run.

When Luke biked over to Ash Acre on Wednesday morning, everyone else was already there – including a very excited-looking TAFKAG with his guitar. But Benny Webb wouldn't let anyone *think* about music till training was over.

Luke's dad stood and watched the depleted squad do their stuff. After a bit he went into the dug-out, to avoid the mess being dropped by the black redstarts who were nesting in the North Stand roof. Although almost everyone had played the night before, Benny still drove them hard. And when they worked on set-pieces he demanded one hundred per cent effort there too. Which was precisely what he got from Half-Fat – who hurtled in so fast to get on the end of one of Luke's teasing free kicks that he smashed into a post and had to retire hurt.

To finish, there was a short practice match. But with Terry off the pitch attending to Ruel and Half-Fat, there were hardly enough players to make a game worthwhile. "There you go, son," cried Benny, lobbing a blue bib to TAFKAG in the dug-out, "Get out here and make up the numbers."

The next twenty minutes weren't easy for Luke. His dad wasn't much cop at music. But he was a whole lot better at that than he was at football. The last time Luke had played with him he'd been three – on the beach at Eastbourne. He hadn't seemed too bad then. In fact he used to say he'd once had a trial with Albion. Maybe he'd meant *on* trial. Whatever – he was criminally poor now.

OK, it *was* hard to play serious football in crushed-velvet loon pants. And TAFKAG's Alice-band kept flying off, so his hair got in his eyes. But he only made contact with the ball four times – and two of those were when he went to fetch it from behind the Town End goal after miscued clearances from Gaffer.

But then again, TAFKAG didn't make his living by hoofing a ball about. And the people who did weren't performing to a very high level at all. Only Luke and Frederick were playing well. And since they were on opposite sides, they completely cancelled each other out. So when Benny blew for full time the scoreline read the same as on the night before: nil-nil.

"Have you lot got an allergy to scoring or something?" shouted the Shaggy Supremo as Madman rolled the ball over to him to take inside. But instead of bending to pick it up, Benny lashed it with ferocious accuracy back past the startled keeper and into the corner of his net. "*There!*" he roared on. "*That's* what I wanna see more of in the next three matches! Start hitting that flippin' net!"

As they all trooped down the tunnel, Luke saw Neil Veal hovering by the home dressing-room door. That was where he normally hung about, hoping to waylay Luke and Fred. But normally he looked more chipper than this.

"What's up, Vealy?" laughed Narris. "Michael Jackson said he can't make our recording session? Never mind, eh. There's always Madonna. *She*'ll do it!"

"Well, in all fairness," Veal replied, following the players in, "I must admit I haven't been as lucky as I'd hoped to be on this one..."

"No sweat," said Cool F, already setting up a beat-box over in his corner. "TAFKAG's your dude. We worked up a number on the road to Cardiff."

"Right on," grinned Luke's dad, still panting from his exertions out on the turf. "We kinda slotted together two bits of songs that we'd already written – just like John Lennon and Paul McCartney used to do, you know?" He strummed a scale on his guitar that had everyone rolling their eyes. "We think it's *heavy*."

"We're all ears," shouted Terry V from the bench where he was examining the still half-dazed Half-Fat. "Give us a blast!"

And they did. TAFKAG on guitar in the middle of the dressing-room floor; Cool F behind him with his beat-box on the bench.

What followed was quite easily the strangest musical experience of Luke's entire life.

It began with his dad picking out a plinky-plonky little tune, then whining this verse straight out of Happy-Hippy Sixties Sound-Heaven:

Come with me down to the fields of Al-bee-on:
Acre of Ashes, and Bovril and pies
Killers of giants and slayers of dragons –
Fairytale players to dazzle your eyes...

Not *too* bad, thought Luke, still holding his breath. It's not one of his *absolute* worst. But then came the next bit, and he had to think again...

Coconut bath-tubs appear in the sky,
Floating in custard and peas
Here come the gerbils with parachutes on –
DOG-MEN SNEEZE!

As everyone's mouths fell open – but before anyone could protest – Cool F switched on his tape. The room was flooded with three booming drumbeats, then to the backing of a deep, churning Massive Attack-style synthesizer riff, Luke's mate's rich, sluggish, utterly menacing voice took over.

"*I...*" he somehow murmured and roared at the same time, "*...am the King...*" Luke felt a brilliant chilling vibe pass through him from the soles of his feet up to the hairs on the back of his neck – and clearly the same thing was happening to every other listener. "*...of the Castle...!*"

"Woo-*Whooo!*" Narris couldn't help yelping. And Chrissie clapped in awe. But the riff powered on, shaking up everything that wasn't nailed down in that crummy old dressing room. "*You're...*" Cool F cranked up the volume still further, pointing a lazy finger at what could only be That Other Lot. "*...the Dirty ... Rascals!*"

That got the whole room cheering and whooping so hard that they barely heard the brief "Don't-You-Mess-With-The-Albion" rap that Frederick threw in before all the noise abruptly ceased, and in came TAFKAG with an even more awesomely unsuitable verse about velvet geraniums and "the duck in the stone limousine". Then, not a micro-second too soon, it was back to Cool F.

"*I...*" everyone joined in this time, "*am the King ... of the CASTLE...! You're...*" they all pointed Manchester-wards "*... the Dirty ... RASCALS!*"

And so it went on – through Frederick's next rap, through TAFKAG's last unreal verse, then into the final massed King-of-the-Castle chant that had even Benny Webb singing along and punching the air with the others. When it was over, Luke's dad took a step back and raised Cool F's arm in triumph. "So what do you say about *that*, then?" TAFKAG beamed at Neil Veal.

"Er – well..." Vealy looked as if he'd just been mugged. Then again, he usually did. "I'd be *very* happy with – um – *parts* of it..."

"No parts, man," Cool F shot back. "Whole package. Nuff said."

"Well ... since I don't actually *have* anyone else in the frame..." Veal began.

"I think we can take that as a yes!" TAFKAG grinned at Cool F, high-fiving him, then fixing his eyes on the cracked ceiling before bawling at the top of his reedy little voice: "*Oh Hell-o Wem-ber-leeee!*"

6

On Thursday after school Rodney was waiting at the gates in his old Escort. Rodney was always there on Thursdays. Luke's mum came every other day – just in case a football manager or agent was loitering with the intention of tempting Luke back into the game. But on Thursdays she had a gardening class, so she sent Rodney to go and ferry him safely home.

Cool Frederick had only been in school since midday, but he was leaving at the same time as everyone else. "Have you done that French translation yet?" Luke asked as they headed up to where Rodney was waiting. "It's a real pig."

"Yeah, safe. Did it in your dad's van on the way back from Cardiff." Luke glanced at him in surprise. His dad was such an awful driver, his passengers were usually too car-sick to talk, let alone put a wodge of French poetry into English (or, come to that, "fit together" a hippie-hop single either). The Cool One dipped a hand into his bag and pulled out his French exercise book.

"Be my guest," he said, handing it over to Luke. "But hey – don't copy *all* of it."

"I won't," said Luke. "Cheers, mate. Oh, and look, thanks for doing my dad that favour with the song too. It's years since anyone's let him near a studio. D'you think they'll really let you do it, though?"

Cool F nodded. "No way they can't."

"You sound pretty confident," said Luke. "And *your* bit was ace. But, well, *Dad*'s part..."

"TAFKAG – nuff respect!" Frederick paused and offered Luke his hand. "A tenner says we get to number one."

Luke felt just a shade disloyal about it afterwards, but he was shaking Cool F's hand and saying "You're on!" before the word "one" was out of his mate's mouth. Ten quid was ten quid, after all.

"Frederick, how are you?" said Rodney through his wound-down window. "Can we offer you a lift anywhere?"

"Nice one," replied Cool F, getting into the back. "I'm on my way up to James Prince's place. Final delivery – right?"

"Oh – *right*," Rodney and Luke said together. They knew all about this. James Prince, multi-millionaire owner of Majestic Software, was no older than Luke and Cool F – and by all accounts a good deal nerdier than both. But there was no doubting the kid's genius when it came to computers. His skills in the software market had already put him high in the Top Hundred of *The Sunday Times* "Rich List". And the eighteenth century mansion he owned up on the Heights outside town was a clear reminder of that fact to everyone who saw it.

Saw it in photos, that is. Few people had ever set eyes on the actual house. It stood inside its own forest, protected by a security system that the US President would have died for. Even fewer people saw James Prince himself nowadays. Reclusive since the age of nine, he communicated with the outside world only by computer screen. According to staff at the mansion, he even spoke with his parents – who lived in the east wing – only through e-mail.

But there were two definite facts about JP that almost everyone knew. One: he didn't get out enough. Two: he was a fanatical supporter of That Other Lot. And Cool F had recently discovered a third: he had weird taste in music. He knew this because the Majestic Boy had hired him to track down the entire set of Eurovision Song Contest winners – on the original discs.

"So you've found all the records now, then?" Luke asked, as Rodney flogged the flagging Escort across town and up the steep hill.

Frederick patted his bag. "Last three in here. Good client. Pays on the nail."

Luke had gone up with the Cool One to make an earlier delivery. They hadn't got any further than the gatehouse. Prince's heavies had seen to that. Luke was disappointed. He'd hoped at least to get a glimpse of the house. There were rumours that the kid had built his own mini Old Trafford over the old tennis courts – and rigged up a computer-generated crowd to cheer and chant while he kicked around inside the little stadium. Nerds*ville*!

"We'll wait and take you back down," said Rodney as he stalled the car outside the towering gates. "You won't be long, will you?"

And he wasn't. Two of Prince's heavies were waiting to take the small package. One made a quick call on his mobile – to give JP's secretary the go-ahead to transfer the last part of the fee into Frederick's bank account. Then Castle Albion's stylish stopper was back in the Escort.

"You never got inside, then?" asked Luke as they clattered back down to town.

"Not till next Monday, no."

"What?"

"Guy's been e-mailing me. We got to rapping 'bout football. He's asked me up to hang loose next Monday night. Wants to play a game, he says."

Luke twisted around. "A *game*! Of football? With James Prince! *You*?"

"And you. I asked if he wanted to meet the

Studless Sensation too." He raised an eyebrow. That was what the tabloids called Luke because he always played in trainers. (His mum had never let him have boots as a little kid, and now he couldn't get used to the studs.) "You *wanted* an eyeful of the place, right?"

Luke gasped. "Right!" He reached behind and high-fived his mate.

"And while you're in there," Rodney couldn't help suggesting, "ask him if he'd like to put up seven million pounds and bail out Castle Albion."

Luke and Frederick winced. If the club had got ten pounds for every time someone had said that in the past week, it wouldn't *be* in debt any more. Princey was just the kind of "local businessman" who was always coming to the rescue of ailing clubs. But most local businessmen don't have "MUFC" tattooed in seven different places on their bodies. There was absolutely *no way* there.

"Yes, Rodney," sighed Luke. "We'll ask for the cash in a suitcase, OK?"

7

"C Albion Squad" were scheduled to record at eight on Friday evening. That's what it said on a board in the studio foyer. TAFKAG had picked up Luke from school then driven straight there. It was now four forty-five in the afternoon.

The old boy was dead nervous. He didn't seem to realize that they were three and a quarter hours early. All he wanted was a room where he could rehearse and "tidy up" his lyrics. Finally a producer found him one, and since it was a warm evening Luke went outside and sat under a tree to do his Physics homework.

After seven-fifteen he began to see the rest of C Albion Squad – plus Vealo – rolling up in the distance. Chrissie had got his hair into dreadlocks for the occasion. Craig, Dennis, Half-Fat, Narris and Carl were all in club blazers – less Boyzone than MiddleAgedzone. Madman – as ever – was in his keeper's kit (and Luke just knew he would have his black-and-white latex skeleton top on underneath).

Luke waved and got on with his circuit diagrams. Only once was he interrupted. A really pretty secretary came over and politely asked if she could have his autograph for her younger brother. Apparently he supported That Other Lot (surprise!) but he'd loved seeing Luke chip his goal against Liverpool in the Sixth Round, and he'd been practising it in the back garden ever since.

"And that guy rehearsing in there?" she asked when Luke handed her the autograph book back. "TAFKAG? He's your *dad*, right? We've been watching him from the mixing room. He's hilarious! Really, *really* funny. We're in fits!"

Luke looked at her, slightly puzzled. Her grin was utterly dazzling and she didn't *seem* to be trying to wind him up. "Right," he said, frowning. "Thanks."

At seven fifty-five Terry V came trotting over. "Come on then, old son," he laughed. "Got your pipes in full workin' order, have you? We're about to go on."

"Is Frederick here yet?" Luke asked as they walked back across the lawn.

"Been 'ere ages. The producer's already started workin' with 'im on his bit. Reckons the kid's a natural. Well – don't we all? Not that I know much about that sort o' music. Gimme jazz any day of the week. Me and Benny both."

"Is Benny coming?"

"You betcha! He reckons everyone in pop music's got money to burn. He's goin' from door to door in there now – tryin' to find someone to buy the club. You oughta see the looks he's gettin'! Makin' 'em an offer they can't understand!"

"D'you think the club's *really* going to go bust?" Luke asked.

"Nah, son – pecker up! Where there's life there's hope. And there's still a bit of life left in some of us. Even old Ruel." He smiled. "Half-Fat's really strugglin' after he crocked himself in trainin', though. And them youth lads are too terrified to tie up their own boots, let alone play." He winked at Luke. "But there'll be someone *new* on the bench for the Plymouth game tomorrow."

"Really? Who?"

Terry just winked again as they went inside. "Come on. You've got a hit to make!"

Because the producer was pushed for time, he did the recording in two separate studios side by side. In one, Cool F did his rap stuff with a band of session musicians, then all the rest of C Albion Squad joined in on the choruses. Meanwhile in the studio next door TAFKAG did *his* solo bits. The laid-back producer said he could splice it all together in no time afterwards.

Cool F was a natural. He even looked like a

popstar already with his shades and his fur-trimmed kagoul hood up. Luke watched in awe as his mate quickly hit a fantastic groove with the band. He recorded at least five versions of his rap – smoothly making up a new one on the spot every time.

But through the big glass wall TAFKAG didn't seem quite so at home. Twice Luke saw him break a guitar string. And he couldn't seem to find a comfortable position to record from. At one point he was even lying flat on the floor. A whole host of studio staff were watching him from the console. And every last one seemed in danger of dying of laughter. Luckily TAFKAG was so obsessed with his own problems that he didn't appear to notice.

By nine-thirty it was all done and dusted. "OK, *OK*, C Albion Squad," called the producer through his mixing-desk mike, "that's wrapped it up. Thanks for your time. We'll have the whole thing in shape by the morning. On Monday it'll be in the shops. Oh and hey – what's the track gonna be called?"

Over in his studio TAFKAG tried several times to answer but his mike had been switched off. Everyone in next door looked at Cool F, who just shrugged and suggested, " 'Castle Rap'?"

" 'Castle Rap' it is, then," said the producer. " 'Castle Rap' by TAFKAG and C Albion Squad."

"Or why not just *C Rap*?" said Madman, flicking up his jersey for a glimpse of latex skeleton. He was sulking because the producer hadn't let him record a selection of aeroplane-engine sounds for the B-side.

TAFKAG got out before the rest and was waiting on the drive by his psychedelic van. As Luke passed through reception, half a dozen people were still laughing. "He's brilliant, your dad!" spluttered one guy with a ponytail. "Go TAFKAG! I'd never heard of him before. How long's he been around?"

"Ages," said Luke. "Different names, though." He tried a few: "Simply Green? Grass Green and the Flowerbeds? Lawn Green and the Herbaceous Borders?"

The half-dozen creased up again. "Magic!" grinned a session drummer once he'd recovered himself. "And I'd never liked alternative comedians before."

"Alternative *what*...?" Luke began, then he felt a hand at his back urging him forward and through the door. Outside he turned to find Neil Veal.

"Sorry! Sorry! Sorry! Hit me now!" said Vealy, closing his eyes and offering up his chin. "I just thought it was safer to say he was a comic." He braced himself.

"But does *Dad* know they think that?" gasped Luke.

"No, no! I swear he didn't twig!" Eyes shut, he was still awaiting his sock on the jaw.

"Go on, give him one from me!" Chrissie hissed in Luke's ear.

"Well he looks pretty fed up about *something*," said Luke, turning to go to him.

TAFKAG was fuming as he bent to change yet another string on his guitar. "All right, dad?" Luke asked nervously. "Were you happy with that, then?"

He wouldn't look up from his re-stringing. "After what happened at the end!"

"*What* happened? Tell me?" He glanced back. Veal's chin was still out.

"They wouldn't use my title, that's what! 'Castle Rap'! Who'll remember that?"

"So what was *your* title?"

Briefly he looked up, over the trees and into the darkening sky. He swallowed hard, then said in a hushed, almost tearful voice: " 'Excerpt From The Diary Of A Fugitive From Venus'."

Even Luke had to bite back a smile then. "Yeah well, that *is* more memorable, I guess." The he heard an irritated "Ow, that *hurt*!" from behind. Chrissie had taken a pop at Vealy anyway – just as a little reminder about Wash and Go.

8

Luke's dad dropped him at Ash Acre at two fifteen the next afternoon. The atmosphere was really weird. Normally for a home game against Plymouth, Albion would be lucky to get a crowd of 3,000. Today, though, there were probably that many outside the ground already.

Admittedly most of them were queuing for Cup Final tickets. And when people did that they usually had a glint in their eye – especially when they laid hands at last on the precious little passports to Wembley. But *these* fans couldn't have looked less excited. All their thoughts were on the three remaining League games – or else on the Pay-Up-Or-Pack-Up deadline that was now only eleven days away. Cup Final? Luke could almost hear them thinking. *What* Cup Final?

It was much the same inside the decrepit old stadium. No one could get worked up about Wembley with such a cloud hanging over the club. There had been another ominous event

41

here the day before too. The black redstarts had all flown away. (REDSTARTS DESERT SINKING SHIP, declared the *Evening Argus*.) Luke felt the tension in the hands that clapped him on the back as he passed through. "Do it for us, Luke," smiled a frail old lady in a housecoat just before he went into the home dressing-room. "We've got to keep going, haven't we?"

"Course we have, Mrs Bowman," Luke smiled. She'd been doing the teas since nineteen fifty-seven. She knew all about keeping going. There were plenty more like her too.

Thankfully the players looked up for it. Most of them were still buzzing after the recording session. (Out of respect for Luke, no one said a word about alternative comedians.) Focusing hard as they got changed, they went through their regular pre-match rituals. Carl Davey had brought an extra-big lucky pineapple for Craig Edwards to hurl at his bottom (to make sure he scored). So big, in fact, that it skewed out of Craig's hand as he threw it – and smacked Terry V on the side of the head as he gave Half-Fat's dodgy leg a last look over.

"Hey steady on," Terry said, putting a hand to his greying temple. "I'm meant to be playin'. Take me out and we're down to ten before we even get started."

"Ah, no worries," laughed Narris. "You've been smacked on the head by the Pineapple of

Destiny. *You're* bound to score now!" Carl just scowled.

"So where's this new face on the bench then, Terry?" asked Gaffer. "It's nearly time for the off." Luke looked up. Obviously word was out about the new guy.

"Benny's giving him a guided tour of the trophy-room, is he?" joked Madman.

Terry stopped rubbing his temple and just tapped his nose. "You'll see in a minute. I'll tell ya this though – he'd give *you* lot a run for your money."

Then the door opened and C Albion Squad prepared to meet its latest recruit. But it was only Benny – wrapped-up as ever in sheepskin. A chorus of *"Doh!"* greeted him. "Where is he, Boss?" piped Chrissie. "Where's this new sub?"

Benny didn't reply at once. A faint smile crossed his face. Somebody had to be the first to notice – it happened to be Frederick. Cool F simply pointed at the hem of Benny's coat. Under it, instead of his usual grey slacks and Hush Puppies he was wearing white Albion socks and a pair of boots.

"Flippin' heck Boss," Dennis yelled on behalf of everyone else. "It's *you*!"

Benny's face grew so menacingly solemn that his beard seemed to bristle out to twice its normal size. "Too right it is!" he told them all. "I'll be on that bench today – *and I want you to* do everything humanly possible to stop me from 'aving to come on! *You're* the kings of this castle! Now get out there and knock that Plymouth lot for six! Put the *Arghh* back into Argyle!"

Luke felt fairly stunned as he ran on to the pitch. So did the South Side fans when they saw Benny kicking in with his sheepskin coat on. For a moment they fell completely silent. Then, taking their lead from Supporters Club Chairman and choirmaster-in-chief Rocky Mitford, they burst into:

"One Stanley Matthews! There's Only One Stanley Matthews!"

The players couldn't help grinning. The great Stanley M – Stoke and Blackpool's "Wizard of Dribble" – had played at the top level till the age of fifty. Benny wasn't *quite* that old but he wasn't far off. And he'd never played at the top level either. Four hundred and sixty-nine times he'd turned out at centre-half for Swindon, Millwall, Grimsby, Crewe and finally the Albion. He'd never won a thing except the respect of his team-mates and each club's fans (which *he* always said was the best prize of all). But to come back *now...*

Maybe, though, he wouldn't have to. Straight from the off, Albion pressed forward. Chrissie seemed to have aerodynamic Brylcreem on his hair: he was really flying down his flank. Terry too was looking a lot sharper in his second game back. And in the fourteenth minute they combined to put Albion ahead.

Chrissie raced on to a through-ball from Luke, beat his man to the byline, whipped in a near-post cross... And there was Terry to flick home his first goal in nine years. And he used *just* that part of his head that Craig had belted with the pineapple! Even Carl had to run up and give him a hug for that – as the fans on the South Side flung their own big inflatable fruits in the air.

Plymouth hit back as best they could. Twice Madman had to parry close-range shots. And once Gaffer cleared off the line at full stretch. But as the half wore on, Luke took the game by the scruff of the neck. A breathtaking save from the Plymouth keeper kept out one of his trade-mark chips, and on the stroke of half-time he put Narris clean through on goal, only to see his shot thud into a post.

"We should be more than one up," Benny told them back in the dressing room. "They look nippy on the break. But as long as we're winning I won't come on."

When the team reappeared from the tunnel, Rocky and the South Siders gave the Sour-faced Supremo a blast of:

"Benny, Benny, Show Us Your Legs!"

Then Luke grabbed hold of the game again and – tackle for tackle, pass for pass – he had his most masterful forty-five minutes for Albion. But apart from one Cool F volley that shaved the bar, the boys in blue and white never really looked like scoring again. Luckily neither did Plymouth. Until the eighty-eighth minute.

Then Half-Fat took a short ball from Dennis just in front of the home dug-out. His control let him down, the ball bounced off his shin, and when he turned to chase it, he twisted his gammy leg and fell in agony. His number was up for that afternoon. As he was stretchered off, Benny stood and de-sheepskinned.

"He's Fat! He's Round! He Wouldn't Cost A Pound!"

roared Rocky's lot. But there was warmth in their abuse. *And* a great big dollop of sheer disbelief.

Gaffer pushed up to take Half-Fat's place in midfield. That made room for Benny to slot into his old berth in central defence. Thirty seconds later, as he went in to make his first challenge on the edge of the box, it was as if the clock had been turned back twenty years – worse luck for Albion.

Twenty years before, the Boss's tackle on Plymouth's number ten wouldn't have raised an eyebrow anywhere in Ash Acre. That was then. Now the laws were much, much tighter. As the striker writhed about on the deck, every other Plymouth player and all the travelling fans raised their voices in outrage. And quick as a flash the ref raised his yellow card at poor old Ben.

The number ten recovered at once, asked for the ball, and squared up to take the free kick. Madman positioned a pretty solid wall in front of him – but not quite solid enough. Somehow the dirty rascal in green and white blasted his kick *between* Carl and Narris. Madman dived low to block it, but before he could scuff the ball away to safety, in danced their gleeful number eight to poke it into the net.

One-one. And that's how it stayed for the game's last few seconds.

"Goin' Down, Goin' Down, Goin' Down!" jeered the Plymouth faithful as Albion trudged off with bowed heads. This is as bad as it gets, thought Luke. Some hopes! Worse news came through as they slumped down in the dressing room: Exeter had won. Albion were now three points adrift.

9

On Sunday morning TAFKAG drove Luke back to his mum's.

He had a lunchtime gig at the Art Of The Possible pub, so he'd perked up a bit after his disappointment over the song-title. But that wasn't all. Neil Veal had got hold of an advance promotional pressing of *Castle Rap*. That morning he'd rung TAFKAG and Luke, and played it to them over the phone. It sounded all right. Ridiculous yes, but . . . all right. Apparently Chris Moyles and Zoe Ball at Radio One thought so too. It was going straight on to their playlists!

"I can't understand it," grinned TAFKAG in the van. "Zoe Ball's always saying she supports That Other Lot. Why should she do *us* a favour?"

"Must be a glory supporter," muttered Luke, staring out of the window. "Besides, she's got to play great music – whoever it's by." Then silently he prayed that the DJs didn't make it *too* clear that they thought it was a joke record.

Luke himself didn't feel much like laughing as

that day dragged on. His mum made an awful hash of the lunch, but that happened every week. What was new was the slowly creeping feeling that maybe Albion *were* going to go down. Or else go out of business altogether. Either way, doom seemed to be looming. It made Luke sick to the pit of his stomach. Even so, he knew that for him it wasn't half as desperate as it was for Gaffer, Dennis, Narris and all the rest. They depended on the club for their livelihood. For weeks now they'd hardly been paid any wages. The worry of that – on top of everything else – must have been driving them potty. Or in Madman's case, pottier than he already was.

On the field, Albion had just two games left to turn things round. Both were at home, which was a plus. First they had Scunthorpe on Tuesday night. Then – and every time Luke thought about this, he went dizzy – on the season's last Saturday they entertained the only other candidates for the drop: Exeter City!

The League table on the screwed-up page of the *Sunday Mail* in the swing-bin told its own grisly story. Luke and Rodney kept sneaking into the kitchen to take a peek at it. But however many times they looked, the figures didn't change. Exeter now had just one game left. They were three points ahead of the Albion and they'd scored six more goals. What it boiled down to was this:

To stand any chance at all of staying up, Albion *had* to get a result on Tuesday night. A win would put them level on points with Exeter. But unless they scored six – which they hadn't done for four seasons – they would still be behind on goals scored. That meant they would have to gun down Exeter at the Last Chance Saloon on Saturday. What a game *that* would be! But first they had to get that result against Scunthorpe – which wouldn't be a piece of cake. Scunny were going for the play-offs themselves, so they'd be giving it their all.

It was just as well that Luke's Albion-mad headmistress had written to his mum, asking permission for him to attend a "special evening class for high-flyers on aspects of iron". It wasn't a complete and utter fib. Luke's mum didn't know that "the Iron" was Scunthorpe United's nickname.

"Why *do* you keep poking about in that bin?" she snapped now, breezing suddenly into the kitchen.

Both Luke and Rodney stood to attention. "Oh, I'm just scraping the lunch plates, Mum," said Luke. He snatched up his plate from the draining board and tipped a large uneaten portion of burnt lasagne into it.

"Haven't you two done the washing-up yet? My, you're taking your time!" Then, unexpectedly, she smiled. "I've just been on the phone to my gardening-class tutor. We were going to have a wine-and-cheese party at his house on Tuesday. But his wife's fallen ill with the flu. So I offered to hold it here instead." Her smile hardened. "Naturally, I'll want you both to help me out. Taking coats, pouring drinks, getting little sausages out of the oven. I'll be so tied up with my guests that I won't be able to attend to all of that."

"Tuesday?" Rodney answered with a quiver. "Would that be Tuesday *evening*?" She nodded. "Ah – well of course, dear, *I'd* be delighted to do what I can. But Luke – as you'll remember – has a prior engagement."

"A prior engagement? What are you talking about?"

"You know, Mum," Luke put in, feeling his face go bright red. "The headmistress wrote you a note. The – um – evening class?"

"Oh *that*!" She waved a hand in the air. "Don't you worry about that. I haven't replied to her yet anyway. You don't want to sit and be bored about iron. No, I need you here. We'll all have a lovely time – you'll see."

"But Mum! I—"

She glared at him, her smile evaporating. "No buts, Luke! I have ... asked ... you ... to help ... me ... out! Do I make myself clear?"

"Yes, Mum. It's just that..."

"*It's just that NOTHING!* You're already going into school for extra IT *tomorrow* evening." That was Luke's excuse for his visit with Cool F to James Prince's place. "And then you have that trip to the Peak District in two weekends time!" (Another note from the headmistress, to make sure he got away for the Cup Final – the "Peaks" being Wembley's twin towers). "If that school has its way, I'll soon forget what you look like! No, young man, you'll stay here on Tuesday and that's final!" Then she turned on Rodney. "And you – when *are* you intending to do the washing-up? It's nearly time for tea!"

"Oh... er..." Rodney dithered, rummaging in the larder. "I can't seem to find the pinny, dear. You know – the pink one?"

"There's a new yellow one," she said, turning on her heel.

"Yes dear, I can see that. But I rather *like* the pink one. I always use that one."

"Not any more you won't," she called over her shoulder. "It's well past its best. I bundled it up with some of those ghastly old shirts of yours and took the lot down to Oxfam yesterday."

Rodney turned to Luke, bug-eyed with panic behind his glasses. "The pinny!" he hissed. "The lucky pink pinny! How can we win the Cup without it?"

Luke shrugged. It didn't, to be honest, seem like the biggest of their problems.

Cool F and Luke were due at Majestic Towers at seven thirty on Monday evening. They got there on the dot, both already in their kit, and the heavies on the gate radioed through to Miss Estella Sanchez, James Prince's personal assistant. "Miss Sanchez is waiting at the end of the drive, sirs," said one. "Under the monkey-puzzle tree. Enjoy your visit. Oh – and good luck in the League."

They strolled up the wide, winding drive for what felt like an hour. The further they went, the thicker the forest around them became. There was no sign of any house. No sign of any life at all – except for jabberings from various sorts of wildlife. Luke's mum would have loved it. There were sure to be ha-has here. Rodney would have had a field day too with his bird-spotting binoculars.

Then he heard Cool F whistle under his breath as he did some spotting of his own. There beneath the monkey puzzle. This had to be

Estella Sanchez – dressed in a tight black tracksuit with her long blonde hair tied back, and an electronic clipboard under her arm. Maybe James Prince was a nerd, but he was a nerd who knew what to look for in a personal assistant.

"Mr Prince is waiting for you at the stadium," she smiled, turning at once to lead them down a smaller path. "You will have five minutes with him – maximum. He has to be at a three-way Virtual Conference with Los Angeles and Delhi at eight o'clock. A few words of advice: you may call him Mr Prince, if words need to be exchanged. He prefers not to hear the words 'Liverpool', 'Leeds United', 'Chelsea', 'dandruff' or 'Microsoft' in open conversation." She paused then lowered her voice. "And it might be advisable to let him ... win."

Luke and Frederick exchanged glances. "Will you be playing too?" Cool F asked.

They both saw her stiffen a little before she answered. "No, Mr Prince wishes me to be the referee."

Then Luke almost jumped out of his skin as a monumental din erupted from the forest's deep silence. It took him a moment to realize it was a football crowd. A far bigger crowd than any he had ever played in front of. But as if with one voice it was singing: "*Come on Princey! Come on Princey!*"

"What the. . .?" Luke began to shout. As he did so, the crowd noise miraculously softened. Then as he closed his mouth it swelled up again.

"That's Mr Prince's Virtual Attendance Tone. VAT for short," Miss Sanchez explained – every one of her words crystal clear. "It's voice-sensitive."

Then the trees thinned and they found themselves facing a great brick-built, slate-roofed bunker. That was where the sound was coming from. "Welcome to Old Trafford," smiled Miss Sanchez, stepping aside. Pressing a button on her clipboard, she made an invisible door swing open in the wall.

First Cool F, then Luke, then JP's PA stepped inside. Not since those kids went through that wardrobe into Narnia had a bunch of people passed so fast from one world into another. When the door closed behind them, they were *in* a floodlit state-of-the-art football ground. Scaled down of course, but not – it seemed – by very much. You could have played a decent six-a-side game on that brilliant green Astroturf pitch. The goals at each end were a good size too.

And the stands! On all four sides, a 50,000-plus crowd was filling them up in glorious multi-coloured 3D. Luke had never been to Old Trafford but he'd seen inside it often enough on TV. (Who hadn't?) And this was it! All canti-levered roofs, hospitality boxes and – over there by the tunnel – even a Virtual Alex Ferguson, grimly chewing gum and shaking his fist at the pitch. All that was missing was the *maker* of this marvellous mini-Theatre of Dreams.

The VAT-register rose by another few decibels: *"He's a Winner! He's a Star! He's a Prince – A Prince Among Men!"* And out of the tunnel – half-running, waving, holding a football – came ... James Prince?

Luke blinked to check that it wasn't just another 3D illusion. But this was a real person, all decked out in the very latest Other Lot kit – even if his glasses, knobbly knees, deathly-white skin, ratty hair and tattoos (two visible) meant that you wouldn't exactly have mistaken him for David Beckham.

Without even glancing at his guests he jogged up to the centre spot, already looking out of puff. As Miss S quickly backed off the pitch, he slapped down the ball and got ready to kick-off to himself. "It's him against you two," Miss S called over. "Remember: he likes to win." She pressed a button and a whistle rang out, then the crowd's roar became almost deafening.

Luke and Cool F grinned at each other, then watched JP kick-off by tapping the ball from his right foot to his left.

That sounds easy. It *is* easy. But for the Twenty-fourth Richest Bloke In Britain it turned out to be a monumental challenge. Twice he missed it altogether. The third time he scuffed it so far sideways that he had to charge halfway to the touchline to get it back.

Again the two Albion stars looked at each other. This was football, but not as they knew it. What were they supposed to do? Tackle him?

Within five seconds JP had answered the question. He began a dribble towards their goal. It wasn't a pretty sight. Even at the age of three, on Eastbourne beach, Luke had been better at keeping the ball under control. First Prince kicked it way too far. Then when he caught up, he trod on it and skidded right over.

Luke and Frederick could only gape in amazement. But on he came, and the closer he got to their goal the louder the crowd cheered. Then from twenty yards, he coiled back one gangly leg and took a shot on the run. *Major* miskick. The ball bobbled away from him but at least it was bobbling in the right direction. Luke and Cool F exchanged glances for a third time. Either one of them could have walked over, trapped it, then turned to start their own attack.

But Luke caught Miss S's eye too. *He likes to win...* Well, Luke wasn't going to rig a result for anyone. But maybe they *could* just give Master Nerd a goal start? Cool F was obviously thinking the same way. They both pretended to lunge for the ball, it rolled on between them, crossed the line and limped into the net.

Neither boy was prepared for what came next. Miss S pressed a button for three blasts of a whistle. *Full time!* The crowd went beserk – so did old VirtuAlex, leaping and dancing for all he was worth. Meanwhile the "matchwinner" somersaulted clumsily all the way back down the pitch in a goal-celebration routine that he had clearly been practising. And when he got to the tunnel, he disappeared down inside it – and that was that.

"Thanks, chaps," said Miss S, buzzing the outer door open again. Luke and Cool F obediently trooped back into the daylight. "You know your way out now. Mr Prince really enjoyed that." She smiled at Frederick, rather more warmly than before. "He'll be in touch again by e-mail. Be seeing you."

Then off she waltzed, and the boys – chuckling now – strolled back down to the gatehouse. There they found one of the heavies standing with what looked like a shoebox under each arm. "For you, sirs," he smiled, handing them over. "Mr Prince wanted you to have them. Just a new little sideline of his. You've heard of Game Boy? Well this is Game James. You've got the lot in there: colour screen, printer, camera. They won't go on the market for another six months. Enjoy!"

"Crucial," grinned Cool F as they passed back out into the real world.

"You said it!" laughed Luke.

11

Luke's mum's gardening party started at eight – half an hour after Albion kicked off against Peterborough.

Luke was trembling all over as he took the last guest's coat up to the spare bedroom. Faintly he heard the crowd noise wafting down from Ash Acre. He should have been *there*, in his kit, on the pitch. Not prancing about in here in a stiff white shirt and black bow tie. He could hardly bear to think of what might happen that night. Albion *had* to draw to stand any chance of staying up. And even then they would have to beat Exeter on Saturday too.

When he came back down to the kitchen Rodney was faffing around in his own white shirt and black tie. He'd served the first round of drinks, so now he was having a quick breather. "I didn't have a chance to tell you before," he whispered, "but I had a call from Mr Mallard at seven fifteen." Luke blinked. Mr Mallard was the code-name Benny Webb used whenever he rang the house. "They were short of one sub tonight – young Darren Hiron had a panic attack and refused to go on the bench. So Mr M gave your name to the ref instead."

"Fat lot of good that is!" Luke hissed back, trembling even more from sheer frustration and – for once – quite a bit of bottled-up anger too.

Rodney shrugged helplessly. He'd been pretty helpless ever since Sunday. The Pink Pinny Business really had hit him for six. He'd even been to Oxfam to try to get it back. But – just his luck – someone had already been in and bought it.

Luke's mum appeared in the doorway. "We're getting peckish in here," she announced. "How long are those *vol-au-vents* going to be?"

Rodney glanced at the oven timer. "Two minutes. We'll be right with you!"

"Don't dally. We want them while they're nice and hot." Then she was gone.

As soon as the timer-bell rang, Rodney scooped them out with an oven glove on to the platter that Luke was holding. "See how those go down," he said.

With a sigh Luke took the stupid little things through to the sitting room. Just inside, a fat woman in a short dress was sitting on the arm of the sofa. "Ah!" she cried, her eyes lighting up, "*Finger foods!* Now you're talking!"

Then disaster struck.

It wasn't really Luke's fault. Greedily the woman grabbed at the platter just as he was about to offer it to her – and sixteen piping-hot pastries fell straight on to her flabby thighs. The noise she made was vile. So was Luke's mum's shriek when she rushed over. "Go and get the wine!" she blared at Luke, snatching up the *vol-au-vents*. "Poor Mrs Fairchild needs a drink after that!"

Luke traipsed to the kitchen, took an opened bottle of Liebfraumilch from the fridge and lugged it back in. "Poor" Mrs Fairchild was still huffing and puffing on the arm of the sofa. Luke had to bend over her to reach her glass on the little table. Unfortunately, as he did so, he let the bottle tilt – and an icy stream of German wine cascaded all down her front.

"Right that's *it*!" screamed his mum, ripping the bottle away and pointing up the stairs. "Go to your room! Stay there! And if I see you again before morning, I'll ground you for the rest of the year!"

OK, thought Luke. OK! If that's how you want it! And even before he was halfway up the stairs, a bold new plan had begun to form in his mind.

He locked himself in his room, tuned into the local radio station at the lowest volume, then quickly changed into his kit. The news from Ash Acre wasn't good. With twenty-five minutes left, Albion were trailing by a goal to nil. And

Benny Webb – on from the start – was having a torrid time. Once again he'd given away the free kick that had led to the goal. Once again he'd been booked.

As soon as Luke was changed, he opened his bedroom window and crawled out on to the bathroom roof. It wasn't too far to jump down from there. And the grass below broke his fall. This was all so risky – but what else could he do? After unlocking his bike and wheeling it out of the side entrance, he had to pass the bay window of the sitting room. He was fairly sure no one spotted him. At least no one came out and yelled at him to stop as he pedalled away up the hill.

If the floodlights hadn't been on, you would hardly have known a game was being played. Even when Luke locked his bike in the players' and officials' car park the ground was deathly quiet – except for the occasional gloating chant from the travelling Scunthorpe fans down at the Town End.

"Luke!" cried a yellow-coated steward behind him as he raced towards the players' entrance. "Blimey – do we need you now!"

"Is it still only one-nil?" Luke asked over his shoulder. The guy nodded.

Once inside, Luke stormed through the empty corridors, up the tunnel and into the full floodlit glare of that seedy but oh-so-special old arena.

Rocky and the South Siders spotted him straight away.

"Studless! Studless!"

they roared in appreciation. Everyone on the pitch looked his way too. And the moment Benny "Wizard of Drool" Webb clapped eyes on him, he set off for the touchline.

It took him quite a while to get there. He looked as if he'd been playing for eighty-one hours, never mind eighty-one minutes. By the time he arrived, the ball was dead and the League's youngest player came on to replace its oldest.

"Luke...!" Benny gasped, gripping his shoulder. He was just too exhausted to say another word. But his desperate eyes fixed on the boy's. That said it all.

"I'll give it my best shot," Luke smiled, then sprinted off into the fray.

It took him a few minutes to adjust to the pace of the game. In the eighty-third he was dis-possessed in the centre-circle, and Scunthorpe almost snatched a second goal from the attack that followed. But by the eighty-seventh, he was truly up to speed: threading an unstoppable ball through the eye of a needle for Carl to run on to and hammer past the keeper. *Goa...!* No!

A full-back on the line dived in to palm it round the post. The ref had no hesitation. Once he'd red-carded the offender, he pointed to the spot. Everyone in blue and white knew who had to take the penalty. Up stepped Luke.

Pressure? What pressure? This lad had scored the winner in the semi-final shoot-out against Arsenal. He didn't plan to miss this one. And he didn't. One-one!

In the last minute Luke nearly won it with a twenty-yard volley that the keeper somehow managed to catch at full stretch. But when the ref blew for time, Albion had the lifeline they needed. A point. A precious point. Now if they just beat Exeter on Saturday they could drag themselves up off the bottom.

Luke had no time to think about any of that, though. He ran off the pitch and didn't stop running till he reached the car park. Pedalling furiously home, ahead of the departing fans, he prayed harder than he'd ever prayed before that his mum hadn't found out that he'd gone AWOL.

The party was in full swing when he got back. Ducking past the bay window, he saw "poor" Mrs Fairchild (soaked, scalded and by now quite clearly pickled as well) leading a conga-line around the sitting room. Luke was up the bathroom drainpipe in a trice, through the open window into his room... And then with an Old Trafford-sized sigh of relief, he fell backwards on to his bed.

Moments later there was a soft tap at his door. "Psst!" said Rodney from outside in a hushed, excited voice. "I just made a quick call to the *Castleline*. We got a draw! One each. I didn't catch who scored our goal."

Still breathless, Luke closed his eyes at the ceiling – and smiled.

12

Benny Webb liked to keep the players on their toes. They never quite knew what to expect at a training session. Sometimes after a win he would make them train extra-hard. Then after a bad defeat he might give them the morning off. But no one – from Luke and Frederick to the now nearly-fit Ruel and Half-Fat – could have predicted what happened on the morning after the Scunthorpe game.

When everyone was changed and waiting to get out on the pitch, Benny backed slowly into the dressing room – carrying an enormous crate of brown ale!

"Steady on, Boss," gasped Dennis. "We only *drew* last night!"

Benny dumped the crate in the middle of the room and straightened up. "All right, lads – help yourselves. Let's bond. There's a lot more to this game than running and kicking. You can't just keep on playing football."

"Well *you* certainly can't, Boss," laughed Narris.

"I'll pretend I didn't hear that. No – at this stage of the season, what really matters is team spirit. And next Saturday it'll all be down to character..."

Terry nodded. "Keeping your nerve."

"Showing *bottle*!" Madman quipped, whipping one out of the crate, holding it up, then opening it with his teeth. After that, everyone else piled in.

"Hey, what about Luke and Frederick?" asked Gaffer. "They're under age."

"Oh, right," said Benny, digging into both sheepskin pockets, throwing Luke a bottle of Charlie Chalk Coke, Cool F a big bag of sherbet, and even finding a pork pie for Madman. Then he sat down and opened a beer for himself.

"You haven't got any Carling Black Label, have you, Boss?" asked Chrissie, wrinkling his nose at the brown ale's taste. "I'm more of a lager man myself."

"Use it for shampoo, then," Carl smirked. "Beer's good for the hair. Or are you now under contract to Wash and Go not to use any other product?"

"Like flip I am," moaned Chrissie. "I dunno what that Veal *does* all day long."

"Well, he's got our record on Top of the Pops

on Friday," Benny revealed to a roof-raising cheer. "TAFKAG rang and told me last night. He tried ringin' you too, Luke, but he said there was a party goin' on and he couldn't get Rodney to understand what he was sayin'. But it's selling like fury, the single. They're gonna play it on Top of the Pops and show clips from our Cup run."

"It's on the radio all the time too," Craig chipped in. "Every time they play it, the DJs fall about laughing. What does old TAFKAG think about that, then?"

Benny took a swig from his bottle. "It did puzzle him a bit, it's true. But *he* thinks they reckon *Frederick*'s bit's funny. No offence there, Frederick."

"None taken," murmured the Cool One between licks of his finger.

"So anyway, Boss," Half-Fat called over from the physio's bench, "on a *slightly* more serious subject: are we gonna beat this wind-up deadline or not?"

Benny frowned hard. "As of this moment in time, I would have to say... No."

"I can't *believe* this!" shouted Dennis over the quadrophonic groaning. "Clubs always get saved! Someone always pays up at the last minute."

"Not necessarily," said Ruel, who had a longer memory than most. "Don't forget

Accrington Stanley. And Workington Town. And Aldershot. And Newport County..."

"But that was in the olden days!" howled Chrissie (who thought anything before the Prodigy's first single was ancient history). "This is *now*!"

"And right now," Benny said, even more solemnly, "no one is willin' to pay a penny to keep Castle Albion in existence. That's the honest truth."

A grim silence followed. Then Cool F took a hand. "Hey," he began, "I wasn't gonna mention this, but the dude that Luke and I went to see on Monday...?"

"James Prince?" said Terry. "Yeah, you told us before the game last night."

"...well, he e-mailed me today. Invited *all* of us up to his pad for a six-a-side. Tomorrow night at eight. And man, that guy's loaded..."

"Filthy rich!" Luke cut in. "He gave us about three hundred quid's worth of hardware just for watching him score a goal. Good stuff too, eh Frederick?"

"Rockin'," Cool F nodded. "So maybe, Boss, if you asked him *real* nice..."

"...he'd break open his piggy bank and hand over seven million!" snorted Narris. "Get a life! Why would he do a thing like that?"

"Why does *anyone* rich get involved with football clubs?" Craig asked, more thoughtfully.

"It's just what rich blokes do. It's like buying toys."

"It *might* be worth a try," said Carl, warming to the idea. "He must be interested in us – to invite us up there in the first place. And *I'd* like one of them Game Jameses too. Anyway, what have we got to lose by going?"

"Someone might get crocked?" suggested Terry. "We've hardly got eleven fit blokes for Saturday as it is."

"No danger of that," Luke assured him. "It's strictly non-contact. The whole game will only last about half a minute – if we let Mister Majestic score."

"Well I say we do it!" cried Gaffer, whose opinion in these things counted. "What else did he say in his e-mail, Fred? Just be there at eight?"

Frederick swallowed some sherbet before nodding his head. Luke could see that there *was* something else. Something he wasn't sharing with them – yet.

But Luke trusted his best mate. So before anyone could quiz the Cool One harder on the details, he distracted them by saying, "And *I* can be there 'cos I'm with my dad tomorrow. Tomorrow *and* Saturday. Oh yeah, I think it's *well* worth having a crack at James Prince. He could be the one: the answer to our prayers!"

13

"With all due respect, Miss," Benny stormed, "whaddaya mean: *it was all in the e-mail*? My lads dunno anything about that! And I've got very strong reservations indeed about going ahead under these conditions."

Estella Sanchez gave the Albion Supremo a strange half-smile. "It *was* in the e-mail," she said. "I know, because Mr Prince asked me to compose and send it." She adjusted her electronic clipboard, then looked behind Benny at Cool F and smiled more broadly. "Perhaps you were only given an *edited* version of the message? But, Mr Webb, it's not such an outrageous request, is it?"

"Maybe not," Benny shot back, as the VAT crowd-noise ebbed and flowed all around them. "But it could do serious psychological damage to my lads."

"What's the prob, Boss?" asked Terry. He stepped across from the gang of tracksuited Albion players who were marvelling at the

VirtuAlex in JP's indoor Old Trafford. "You'll never guess what – if you give the right command, you can get that 'ologram of Alex Ferguson to chuck tea cups about!"

"Mr Webb is concerned about the kit arrangements," Miss S explained.

"They've put us in two teams," Benny added, "and one can wear Albion shirts but the other's got to put on a set of That Other Lot's kit!"

Terry grinned. All the players had followed him over now. "Well, who's in the Other Lot's team?" he asked.

Quick as a flash, Miss S reeled off the names: "Luke, Frederick, Chrissie, Madman, Ruel ... and of course Mr Prince himself – when he arrives."

"Nice side," nodded Terry. He turned to the players. "Well, do any of you lot object to wearin' the enemy's colours for a little kick around here?"

"*Nah!*" chorused the five guys in question. Madman already had his tracksuit top off, and was digging into the basket at Miss S's feet for the Schmeichel-shirt to slip over his skeleton.

"I'm still not sure about this," Benny frowned as everyone got changed – and Carl handed Craig a little plastic pineapple to bung at his bottom. "And how long's the game, Miss? A couple of these fellas are only just back from injury."

"I'm afraid I can't say," Miss S told him. "Mr Prince is expecting a vital call from Buenos Aires. He'll have to leave as soon as it comes through."

Benny walked with her to the touchline, while his players separated out into the two teams. "So where *is* the young man, then?"

At that, the crowd unleashed its *Prince Among Men* chant, VirtuAlex raised an arm in salute, and out of the tunnel came the Kid Who Made Bill Gates Look Cool. Again he completely ignored all the opposition. But now, with the ball under his arm, he went round from Luke to Frederick to Chrissie to Madman to Ruel, energetically shaking their hands and saying "Hi! We can have these!" Up close, Luke saw another three MUFC tattoos. Did this guy *love* That Other Lot!

Then Princey plonked the ball on the centre spot, nodded at Miss S to sound the starting whistle, and kicked off to Ruel. At once the stadium rang with an awesomely loud "*Uni-TED, Uni-TED, Uni-TED!*" Luke *did* feel a bit weird to be wearing the famous Devil-red as Ruel laid the ball back to him. But only for a moment. He saw that JP was heading straight for the "Albion" goal, where Gaffer Mann was playing between the sticks.

Dennis and Craig were both close to Princey, but when Luke played his deft through-ball, they knew what to do. First one then the other "misjudged" the pace of the pass, and let it run through to Princey-Wincey. Suddenly he had only Gaffer to beat. Up went the crowd sound. Down went Gaffer – "anticipating" a shot to his right. And James Prince even had time to adjust his glasses before stroking the ball – off what looked like the sole of his trainer – towards the gaping net. It hit the post first. But what the heck – it went in!

As mayhem broke out among the Virtual Faithful, Prince turned and sped towards Luke, arms aloft, mouth wide open in delirium. It was a terrifying sight. And when he leapt up, coiling his arms around Luke's neck and his legs around his waist, the Studless Sensation almost fell over. But he managed to stay on his feet, and stagger around a bit while the multi-millionaire in his arms screamed: "*Yesss, Yessss, Yessssss, YESSSSSSSSSS!*"

Eventually he got down – and Luke didn't think he'd ever seen a kid look so happy. Again he shook Luke's hand, as if his life depended on it. (This ought to be worth a Princetendo 64, thought Luke. Or even a JamesStation. Maybe it might even tempt JP to fork out seven million and save the Albion.) But when the whistle went, there was only one blast, not three. It wasn't over yet!

Narris kicked off to Carl.

Now Carl had a thing about scoring goals. He just loved doing it: in the League, the Cup, the car park, his mother-in-law's front room. All he really lived for was that moment when he buried the ball then turned to take the acclaim from his adoring fans. And even though he knew the score here (nil-one – and that's how it had to *stay*), his deeper instincts suddenly took over.

He spotted Madman way off his line. The keeper wasn't even looking his way. Instead he was screaming blue murder at the defenders in front of him, just to make his impersonation of Peter Schmeichel seem more lifelike. So, very calmly, Carl drove the ball straight into his goal for the equalizer.

Whacked once again by the Pineapple of Destiny, Carl wheeled away to celebrate. Then he stopped in mid-stride. The crowd had gone dead. Silent. Switched off. It was the creepiest sound Luke had heard since his dad had done a sitar version of "It's Not Unusual" by Tom Jones. Then there were three small bleeps from Miss S. Not the final whistle, but her clipboard-phone ringing.

"Mr Prince," she called out. "Buenos Aires is online. Shall I say you'll be...?"

"One minute," Prince gasped back at her. He stood rooted to the spot, staring at the ball in the back of Madman's net: a perfect kiddies' picture-dictionary definition of the word "gobsmacked".

"Oh *Carl*..." every Albion player said under his breath (with a few *non*-picture-dictionary words thrown in too). This hadn't been the game plan at all. Prince had probably never conceded a goal here before. For a moment Luke was scared stiff he might have them all shot.

But instead he just turned away, dazed, and headed towards the tunnel. And then Miss Tracksuit Sanchez sounded three blasts to end the game. "Hey!" suddenly sliced through the dreadful silence. Benny's voice. Luke watched in amazement as Big Ben came rushing on to the pitch in his sheepskin. "Sir!" He was going to have a go. *Still*. He was going to ask JP to save Castle Albion!

Prince paused as Benny puffed right up to him. "Mr Prince..." He just gave it to him straight: "You wouldn't have seven million quid to spare, would you?"

JP blinked behind his glasses. Benny seemed to be on the point of going down on one knee. Still in his weird trance, Mr Rich's right hand moved to where his pocket would have been if he'd been wearing trousers. He'd thought Benny was asking if he had seven million *on him*! Then his hand dropped again.

"Only you see," Benny began to babble, "our wonderful club – our little *local* club – is gonna go out of existence next Wednesday unless..."

"Mr Prince does read the news on the Internet," Miss S butted in. "He's fully aware of Castle Albion's situation. But, you see, he supports—"

"That Other Lot!" Benny turned to her and snapped back. "I know! I know! But..." But when he turned again to JP, he was drifting once more towards the tunnel. And when he got there, he went inside without looking back.

Miss S buzzed open the door to the forest. "Thanks guys," she smiled. "There are some goodies for you all at the gatehouse. Do keep the red shirts. *Ciao!*"

Luke was the last but one Albion player to traipse out. As he left, he glanced behind for a final look at Virtu Old Trafford. Estella S had called Frederick over. Briefly she touched his arm and whispered something in his ear. Cool F's eyes seemed to pop. What had she told him? Was it about where JP's other three tattoos were?

"Think about it," she suggested with a smile as Frederick followed Luke out.

"Think about what?" Luke asked him when they were back in the forest.

But Frederick just shook his head. "Nothing," he said. "No way. *Nothing.*"

14

"So what will you be doing today?" Luke's mum asked. "Anything special?"

"Don't think so," said Luke, pulling on his trainers. "Just hanging out with Dad."

"I wish you wouldn't use that expression," she scowled, turning to look out of the sitting-room window. It was two o'clock on Saturday May the seventh – the last day of the League season. The steep street outside was teeming with people. Most were in blue and white but a fair few wore red and white too – Exeter fans all the way up from Devon for this most nail-biting of crunch matches. "They look so *fed up*!" Luke's mum laughed bitterly. "It's meant to be enjoyable – isn't it – going to those idiotic games? But that lot look as if they're going to a funeral!"

"Ummm," Luke murmured, pretty grim-faced himself. "Funny game, football."

When TAFKAG pulled up in the van and tooted his horn, Luke dashed out double-quick.

There was always the danger that a passing fan would spot him and say "Have a good one, Luke!" or "Give us a goal today!" and his mum would rumble him good and proper. Rodney came out to the porch alongside her – too nervous about the game even to say goodbye. But when he raised a hand to wave, Luke saw that his fingers were tightly crossed.

It took far longer than usual to get to Ash Acre. There weren't many days when Albion got a capacity crowd for a League game, but this was one of them. A lot of these fans clearly thought there might never *be* another League game here.

And it *was* a bit like a funeral, with the cars crawling along, and the people on foot walking with their heads bowed. Instead of hymns, there were occasional rousing bursts of "*We Love You, Albion* (or *Exeter*)! *Oh Yes We Do...!*" but for most of the time it was ghostly quiet. Luke even saw a few girls in tears – just at the *thought* of their team going out of the League.

Outside the ground, everyone queuing for programmes and at the turnstiles looked haunted. The media were there in force. TV and radio reporters kept stopping people and asking them how they'd feel if Albion went down. "Well, teams come back up from the Conference, don't they?" Luke heard one man reply. "Look at Lincoln. And Colchester. And

Halifax..." "Yeah," put in a passer-by. "But they didn't go out of business too, did they? Like *we* will."

At the players' entrance TAFKAG grabbed Luke by both shoulders and gazed into his eyes. "Sock it to 'em, baby!" he said with passion. He looked as po-faced as everyone else, but Luke knew that inside he was jumping for joy. On Top of the Pops the night before, they'd put some ancient video shots of him into the Albion Cup footage. National Fame! At last! And presenter Jayne Middlemiss had predicted a Top Twenty entry for the single. Even now the public address system was trying to blast out "Castle Rap". And when the tannoy inevitably fizzed, popped and died, ten thousand fans inside kept on singing:

"Velvet geraniums rise from the sea
Turning the night into da-ay.
Watch for the duck in the stone limousine
START TO PRAY...!"

Then briefly they fell apart in a massed fit of the giggles before a rousing chorus of:

"We *Are The Kings Of The Castle!*"

Luke smiled at his proud dad, slipped into Ash Acre and headed on down to the dressing room. It was so strange to think this might be his last-ever matchday walk. In another couple of months all this could be rubble. (Some people said it was rubble already, but what did they know?) The whole ground might be smashed to bits to make way for luxury flats or a row of posh shops. Imagine it – buying Belgian chocolates on what used to be the Town End penalty spot!

Mrs Bowman the tea-lady was outside the away team dressing room. "I'm so on edge, Luke," she admitted. "We've got to win. And it's such a shame that Terry can't use Home Advantage any more." Luke nodded. Terry had used to put the away team off their stroke in all sorts of ways, – fusing the lights, nobbling the heaters, flooding the floor. But after a pack of ferrets had appeared in the Arsenal dressing room before the Cup semi-final, he'd been fingered by the FA and now he was waiting to hear the date of his disciplinary hearing. "I'll do what *I* can though," whispered the little old lady. "I'm thinking of putting a bit of bleach in the Exeter tea at half-time."

Luke grinned and walked through the door marked Home Team. Everyone else was already there, and most of them were changed – including Terry. And Benny. "Don't look at your Boss like that!" Terry laughed. "He's only gonna be on the bench. He didn't think the youth lads could take the strain."

"*Aaaaaarrrrgggggggghhhhhhhhhhhh!*" roared Carl as Craig scored a direct hit with a mushy pineapple that splattered apart on impact.

"I'd like to ram one of them things down his throat," Narris muttered. "If he hadn't flippin' scored up at that kid's mansion, we might have had a new owner by now."

"That's enough of that," Benny said sharply. "We never had a prayer up there anyway. And that's all behind us now. We gotta look ahead."

Just then Cool Frederick looked up from tying his laces and caught Luke's eye. He looked as if he was about to say something, but then decided against it.

"Right then, lads," cried Benny, pulling his sheepskin on over his kit and beginning to pace restlessly around the little room, "This is it! This is the Big One! D-Day – that's D for Doin' In That Lot From Devon! *Right?*"

"*Right, Boss!*"

Benny nodded hard, eyeing each player in turn as he passed. "We've come a long way together, all of us," he went on, "and we've got a long way still to go..." At that moment he trod on a lump of Carl's pineapple, skidded several feet, wobbled, almost steadied himself, then crashed to the floor in a heap.

That certainly lightened the mood. "We *knew* you was on your last legs, Boss!" whooped Half-Fat as Terry helped him up. "Was that a late tackle from the last game or an early one for today?" yelled Chrissie. But amid all the hoots and guffaws, Ruel just narrowed his eyes and said, "Pineapple of Destiny".

"There's not much else I can say after that," smiled Benny, dusting himself down. He closed his eyes, clenched his fists, then thundered on: *"Except get out there and do what you gotta do! All of you! Forget about the Cup! Forget about wind-up Deadlines! Just DIE for Castle Albion FC!"*

Unfortunately for Albion, eleven men nick-named the Grecians were planning to die for *their* cause too – and not just by drinking some dodgy half-time tea. That much was clear even as the two teams ran out to a hugely emotional welcome. Every Exeter player was gritting his teeth so hard that Luke could almost hear the fillings squeak. There was a very real danger that at the end of ninety minutes, the pitch would be strewn with twenty-two corpses. But unless Albion could squeeze out a win before then, it was Hello Football Conference.

Gaffer lost the toss and the men from the West Country kicked off. Straight away they revealed their gameplan. The number nine knocked it sideways to the number eight. He laid it back into the path of the number six, who wellied it high and hard over the roof of the North Stand and into the street outside. Gaffer Mann eat your heart out! He pretended it was a miskick but everyone knew it wasn't. Exeter only needed to draw here to stay up. Nil-nil would do them. So as far as they were concerned, the longer the ball was out of play, the better.

Albion had other ideas though. Luke in particular. The Grecians were playing an ultra-defensive seven-two-one formation, with their lone striker so far away from the rest of the team that they had to send the ball to him by parcel-post. That suited Luke. He soon found he had oceans of space to work in. Again and again he dribbled upfield, unchallenged till he got to the edge of their box. Then he came up against the red-and-white striped wall of resistance.

Three times he managed to slip a sweet ball through: twice to Ruel, once to Half-Fat. But they made their runs too late and Exeter cleared their lines. Both players seemed sluggish after their lay-offs and also – surprisingly – Ruel looked as if he had the jitters. It seemed incredible that a guy who had played for England should be bothered by a game against Exeter City, but the tension was clearly getting to him, and to quite a few others in blue and white – not to mention the poor, long-suffering crowd.

Rocky and the South Siders were trying their level best to lift the team. They kept on chanting:

"One Castle Alb-yon!
There's Only ONE Castle Alb-yon!"

To which the Exeter faithful immediately replied in the same tune:

**"Soon There'll Be None Though!
You're Goin' OUT Of The Window!"**

But the sound they made got thinner and thinner as one Albion attack after another came to grief on the Grecian barricades. And around the half-hour mark, some booing and slow-handclapping began.

When the ball went high into the South Side yet again from an Exeter boot, Luke glanced back at Cool F and scratched his head. The visitors weren't exactly making a game of it but you couldn't blame them. They were fighting for their football lives too. As long as they didn't lose, they were laughing.

Luke gathered the ball from Craig's throw-in, then waved Frederick upfield. His mate went like a whippet at the heart of the Exeter defence. He hadn't got forward like this all afternoon, and suddenly the red and whites panicked. None of them were sure who should pick him up. But while all eyes were on Cool F, Luke just kept coming with the ball. Thirty yards out, he caught a glimpse of the goal. In a single inspired moment he took aim, pulled the trigger and fired.

The ball scorched ever higher towards the top-left corner. Rocky and Co went hysterical. Luke felt his chest go hot, the way it usually did just before he scored. But it wasn't to be. From nowhere the Exeter number three leapt up, got the faintest touch with his head, and deflected the ball on to the post, then away.

That turned out to be Albion's best chance of the half. It was still nil-nil when they trooped inside for the interval. Benny – who had been curiously quiet in the dug-out – just sat shaking his head. "I can feel it slippin' away from us," he said with a face as long as a bloodhound's. "We're not doin' anything wrong. But I just can't see how we're gonna break 'em down."

"Never mind, Boss," Terry V said soothingly. "They're bound to crack in the end. Let's face it – they've conceded seventy-nine in the League so far this season. We'll make it a nice round eighty, you'll see." He handed him his tea. "Here, swig that."

Benny took a mouthful, swallowed half, seemed to go green, then spat the rest out over his sheepskin. Before anyone could speak old Mrs Bowman rushed in – far nimbler on her feet than Half-Fat had been outside. "Ooh, don't touch the tea, anyone!" she gasped. "I've given you the wrong cups!" She pointed at the trayful on the table. "That lot was meant for Exeter. It's got bleach in it!"

When everyone finished laughing, Gaffer said to Benny, "Well you can't keep that coat on now. P'raps it's a sign that you should get out on the pitch."

"Only as an absolute last resort," Benny replied in all seriousness. "I'd much rather you lads did the business for me. But I will come on if I have to."

Ten minutes into the second half, Albion *did* have to make a substitution. Half-Fat was virtually hopping in midfield with his gammy leg, so on came Terry to give things a bit more zip. He linked up well with Luke, and they kept putting Chrissie through to the byline. Chrissie's crosses weren't bad either, but every time he clipped the ball in, an Exeter head got there first to clear it. Ruel and Carl, to be frank, weren't getting a sniff. And as the game entered its last quarter, Albion threw more and more bodies forward as reinforcements. They *had* to convert all this pressure into a goal. They just had to.

Then with eight minutes left on the clock, with everyone except Madman and Gaffer encamped in the Exeter half, and with the 2,000 Exeter supporters making far more noise than the 10,000-plus Albion fans, Ruel got in a tangle with the visitors' left back. Down he went near the touchline, fifteen yards inside the Exeter half. The ref signalled that the Big Guy had been fouled. But that was Ruel's last contribution. Off he limped, and on – to a rumble around the ground that was half-anticipation, half-anguish – came Mr B Webb.

What happened next would go down for ever in Castle Albion folklore. It was all to do with three waves of the hand. The hand of Smart Luke Green.

Luke, placing the ball for the free kick, saw Benny head for the Albion half. The Boss planned to take Gaffer's place at the back, freeing the skipper to move up with everyone else. But that plan didn't appeal to Luke. Benny as Albion's sole defender? He didn't think so. What if Exeter mounted a quick counter-attack? So he waved at his manager, urgently, to run *upfield* instead.

Benny paused and eyed Luke hard. He still looked a bit green from his half-time bleach. Luke just went for it. This was way too important now. Again he waved at Benny to get up into the box. And Benny, almost sheepishly, went.

He was still moving as Luke arrowed in a low free kick. He'd aimed at Cool F, who had made a great near-post run. But Frederick's marker dived in to block his fierce shot on the turn. The ball spun up in the air then plopped down – almost dead – on the edge of the six-yard box. For an instant every single person in Ash Acre froze. Everyone except the still-oncoming Benny Webb.

Do it! Do it! Do it! breathed Luke, going up on his toes. Suddenly, in a tiny oasis of space in the box, it was one-on-one. Benny v the keeper! Both were stretching for the ball – and the keeper, going down hands first, had to be favourite. But before he got his gloves on the thing, Benny slid in – just like he'd slid on the pineapple. And whereas in the dressing room he'd hoofed thin air, now, as he lunged, he gave the ball an *almighty* thwack.

It scorched past the keeper, almost taking his ear off, and nearly went through the roof of the net as well. He'd done it! Exeter had conceded goal number eighty of their League campaign. Albion were in front! And the New Stanley Matthews was buried under ten joyous team-mates – and then a dozen fans too.

Once the pitch was cleared, it was all hands to the pump to keep Exeter out. And this was where Luke's *third* hand-wave came in. Benny trundled back at once to help shore up the defence. Luke had other ideas. One late tackle from the Boss, one free kick given away in a perilous position, and Exeter would be right back in it. "Get up there!" he yelled, waving Benny away to where he'd just had his moment of glory. And this time, he obeyed at once.

The last seven minutes lasted as long as Luke's whole life up to that point. In the dying seconds even the Exeter keeper was up in the

Albion box. But for the Grecians, it wasn't to be. When the final whistle went, and a tidal wave of Albion fans swept on to the pitch, the team in hoops had come up trumps.

Luke just had time to high-five Cool F before both of them were lifted shoulder-high. Albion were safe! Their League status had been preserved for another season. They'd done all the hard work. Now they simply had to find seven million pounds – by twelve noon on Wednesday.

16

Luke woke up that Sunday afternoon on his dad's sofa. He still had all his clothes on from the night before. The night before? Now *there* had been a celebration! Straight after the game, a jubilant Benny had sworn that they would go out and bond like never before. And that's just what they did.

From pub to club to pizza parlour to snooker hall, the entire C Albion Squad – plus what seemed like half the crowd from Saturday's game – painted the town blue and white. Everywhere they went, people bought them rounds of drinks. And since Luke and Frederick were under age, TAFKAG generously kept on knocking back *their* bevvies for them too!

It all came to a soggy end around dawn – in the Tenbury Gardens fishpond. Benny had been "reconstructing" his goal all night – with balloons, inflatable pineapples, snooker balls, rolled-up newspapers, *whatever*. In Tenbury Gardens he was re-living the moment with an empty Kentucky Fried Chicken bucket when Carl, Terry and Rocky Mitford simply picked him up and plonked him in with the goldfish. Madman and Narris then pushed the three of them under the fountain. From there on in it was every man for himself.

Luke and Frederick managed to avoid a ducking, but it wasn't much fun hauling a sodden, sleepy TAFKAG home between them. Especially when he insisted on singing them all the way through the verses he'd left out of the original "Excerpt From The Diary Of A Fugitive From Venus". Finally they got him on to his bed and left him to sleep it off while they both kipped down in the next room.

"Yo!" Frederick now said softly from the armchair as Luke yawned, swung his feet to the floor and rubbed his eyes.

"Hey Frederick," Luke smiled. "Nice night out."

"Kickin'."

"Was that *really* our headmistress in the snooker hall with us?"

"Sure 'nuff."

"Doing juggling tricks with packets of Smoky Bacon crisps?"

Cool F just nodded.

"*Wow!*" came a sigh from the bedroom and TAFKAG staggered into view.

"Hi Dad," grinned Luke. "How's it hangin'?"

"Could be better, son," he answered with a series of winces, as if the words were banging hammers inside his skull. "Could be a *lot* better. But look – did I dream this, or did a group of businessmen *buy* Castle Albion last night?"

"That was some supporters in Pizza Express," Luke said. "They put together a consortium on the spot and pooled all their resources."

"Fab! And how much did they come up with? The full seven mill?"

"Sixty-five pounds and twenty-six pence," said Cool F. "But that included Virgin vouchers."

"Oh." TAFKAG struggled through the curtain to where the cooker stood and somehow rustled up a decent brunch for them all. When they'd eaten it, Luke took a look at him. "Shouldn't you get out of those damp clothes?" he asked.

"Nah. They're drying on me. I'm cool with that." Luke wasn't so sure how cool *he* was with it. There was pond scum all over TAFKAG's yellow satin jacket, and he didn't smell quite as fresh as he might have done. "Now look, guys," he said, "we've got a few hours to kill till the Radio One Chart Show. Why don't I drive us over to Frederick's pad so we can chill and listen to some sounds?"

"Good call," murmured Cool F. "Just change your kit and we're outta here."

* * *

They had a long, slow, relaxing afternoon at Frederick's. The Silky Stopper didn't live in the main house with his sister, but had a fully self-contained little place of his own in the garden. TAFKAG was in seventh heaven as he found one old vinyl album after another that he hadn't heard in years. Luke and Frederick sat with him through The Quicksilver Messenger Service, Blodwyn Pig and Thunderclap Newman, but finally drew the line at the Strawberry Alarm Clock and went to watch a video on the wide-screen TV in the lounge.

"Now that's what I call *real* quality time with my boy," TAFKAG beamed when he emerged. "Hey, let's tune into Radio One then."

"Chart countdown," Cool F agreed, switching from video to radio on a handset.

If C Albion Squad really had hit the chart that week, they weren't anywhere between numbers forty to twenty. But Mark Goodier kept saying that there were five new entries in the Top Twenty. "We'll be one of them!" TAFKAG whooped every time, sounding less and less convinced.

"It's only been out a week, dad," Luke tried to tell him. "I wouldn't get your hopes up too high." But this was a man who *lived* on hope. Hope against all reason. How else could anyone explain the length of his music-biz career?

From numbers nineteen to eleven things

didn't get any easier. Mariah Carey, Five and the Bee Gees all had new entries. "Come on, come *on!*" TAFKAG said through gritted teeth at the wall-mounted speakers. Luke was getting itchy too. He had to be back with his mum by six and it was nearly that now.

Then came the announcement: "*So – as we enter this week's brand new Top Ten, we find not one but TWO soccer singles back-to-back!*" Luke saw his dad go rigid. Albion were in! There were only two football records in the frame: "Castle Rap" and That Other Lot's – and "Reds on the Rampage" had already been out for two weeks. It was just a question now of which one was higher. "*...Get ready for a song like you've NEVER heard before. There used to be a singer who they said Sang The Way Marilyn Monroe Walks. Well, here's a guy who Sings The Way My Dog Eats His Dinner. Just get a load of THIS...*"

TAFKAG shook his head sadly as "Castle Rap" started. "Walk away from it, Frederick," he said. "What do they know about music? *I* think your voice is outta sight." He kept shaking his head as the verse gave way to the chorus. "And would you believe that – The Other Lot are one place higher than us..."

"Dad!" Luke couldn't help spluttering. "Are you still hungover or what! You've got a Top Ten hit! *You!* After all this time – you're a star!"

He jumped across the room and gave the dear old hippie a great big hug. Then they both high-fived Cool F and sang out the rest of the song so loud that his sister Adele rushed across from the house to see what was going on.

TAFKAG – fully sobered up now – took her in his arms, yelled *"We're straight in at number ten!"* and gave her a huge smacker on the lips. It took quite a while to get him out to his van after that, so he could take Luke home. When at last he slid grinning into the driver's seat, Luke turned to Frederick on the pavement. Something had been bothering him ever since Thursday. He had to sort it.

"Look," he said. "If it's personal, you don't have to say a word. But if it isn't, you can tell me – can't you?" He looked his best mate in the eye. "What *did* Miss Sanchez say to you after that game up at James Prince's?"

Cool F swallowed hard, then he leaned closer and murmured his reply.

"Oh I *see!*" Luke gasped, swallowing hard himself. "Sorry! I'm really sorry I brought it up. Sorry – oh *wow!*"

17

Luckily Luke's mum lived on a different planet from most people. By Tuesday evening she still had no idea that Luke had inspired Castle Albion to their life-saving win over Exeter. Nor did she have a clue that her son and ex-husband were now chart stars, thanks to their connection with the club. What she *did* have, however, was one of her weekly killer headaches.

That meant tiptoeing around her till ten o'clock, but then Rodney meekly tucked her up in bed – leaving Luke free to watch whatever TV station he wanted downstairs. Keeping the volume only just audible, he went straight for BBC1. Gary Lineker was presenting a special preview of that Saturday's Cup Final, with help from studio guests Alan Hansen and Trevor Brooking.

"...So we've seen from our clips that Castle Albion *can* play," said Gary. "D'you think they'll be able to produce that kind of form at Wembley, Trev?"

"We-e-e-ll," smiled Mr B. "There's always the danger they might freeze on the day. But in young Luke Green and Frederick Dulac they've got players who – um – *deserve* to play on the biggest stage – and from what we've seen of them so far, they've got the temperament to match their – er – marvellous abilities."

"You're shaking your head there, Alan," SuperGary pointed out with a boyish grin. "You've always said 'You Never Win Anything With Kids'. Would you feel any happier if the whole Albion team was Benny Webb's age?"

"Big Benny won't be in the starting line-up on Saturday," boomed Handsome Hansen. "Ruel Bibbo's fit again and Albion will *definitely* need his big-match experience. But however brilliantly they've done up till now, I *can't* see a side that finished ninety-first in the League beating Man United at Wembley..."

"Ye-e-e-es, but the Cup's a great leveller, isn't it?" Trevor Brooking cut in. "I mean, we wouldn't have given Albion a chance against Villa, Newcastle, Liverpool or Arsenal before *those* games, would we? Yet here they are, through to the Final – and who's to say they can't go all the way?"

"The romance of the FA Cup, eh, Trevor?" laughed Gary. "A real fairytale..."

"But have you *read* any fairytales lately?" asked Hansen, lurching forward in his seat.

"The Brothers Grimm and all that? They're *full* of gory stuff. Limbs hacked off. Blood everywhere." He stabbed his finger in the air. "*That's* what fairytales are about. And *that's* what'll happen to Castle Albion. I say Man U to win by five clear goals. And if they don't win *at all*, then I'll..." For a split-second he couldn't think of a suitable way to go on.

"Streak at Wembley?" asked Trev, quick as a flash.

"Aye! OK! I'll do a streak at Wembley!"

Gary Lineker raised an eyebrow at the camera. "We'll be sure to keep you posted on that one." Then he turned back to Trevor. "You've mentioned Albion's strengths. Are there any special problem areas, would you say?"

"Well, their main one has to be staying in business till the day of the Final. But providing they do that... I mean, it's harsh to single out individuals, but I *do* find their goalkeeper a little – erm – unpredictable." On to the screen came some footage of Madman hurling the ball into his own net at Barnet, then conceding an awful second-half treble against Torquay. "He's probably the best penalty-saver I've ever seen, but in open play he *can* be prone to errors..."

"Well, we understand that he'll be bringing his model aeroplane to Wembley," Gary pointed out. "The one he hangs from the stanchion for luck – and which he *didn't* have for those League games we've just seen. Maybe that'll help?"

"He could bring the whole RAF," said Hansen. "It wouldn't change a thing."

"You seem absolutely convinced about this, Alan," Gary chuckled. "But isn't it true that there are no easy games nowadays?"

"It *was* true," snapped AH. "But that was before this fixture was arranged."

At that point the phone rang. Luke snatched up the receiver fast, before his mum could complain about the noise. "Yes?" he said breathlessly.

"Ah, good evening," said a familiar voice. "This is Mr *Mallard* speaking..."

"Boss! It's me – Luke."

"Oh. Didn't recognize you, son. You watchin' this garbage on the telly? That Alan Hansen ought to be locked up. He gets *paid* to have a go at clubs like us!"

"Don't worry about him, Boss," Luke said as loudly as he dared. "We'll get him streaking at Wembley, you'll see."

"I'm not sure I *wanna* see that," Benny grunted. "But look, that's not why I'm callin'. Terry and me are tearing our hair out here about this flippin' deadline. We've got less than fourteen hours to stay alive. Everyone seems to think *someone* will come in at the last minute.

But, Luke, I'm scared stiff it's not gonna happen. I just can't see who it'll be." There was a crack in his voice; the guy was close to tears. "I really thought our best bet was that James Prince lad. I tried ringin' Frederick just now to see if it was worth havin' one last crack at him. But his sister said he was out deliverin' records somewhere. So what do you reckon, Luke? Is there *any* way we could persuade him to shell out?"

Luke thought long and hard before answering. All he could hear was what Cool F had murmured to him on Sunday evening out in the street. Miss Sanchez's suggestion. Luke didn't think he had ever heard anything so ... outrageous.

But Benny needed an idea from him. A straw to clutch at. And Luke couldn't for the life of him think of anything else. So he shut his eyes tight and said: "Don't blame me for this, Boss. It's what James Prince's PA suggested to Frederick. It's mad. Crazy. Unbelievable that she should even *think* of it. But for what it's worth, what she said was..." And Luke went right ahead and told him.

"I'm sorry, son," Benny said. "You're not speakin' very loud and I think I must've got the wrong end of the stick there. Run that past me again."

Luke repeated the suggestion. Word for word. Benny didn't reply at once.

"That's what I *thought* you said," he admitted. Then before Luke could start to apologize, he went on: "But if that's the only way forward for Castle Albion, then that's the route we're gonna have to take! Cheers for now, Luke." And he put down the phone.

18

Luke was a bit late for training the next morning. Someone had put a rude screen-saver message on the IT teacher's computer, and he wouldn't let the class out till the culprit owned up. But when Luke got to Ash Acre, he realized right away that something was in the air.

For a start there were more than fifty reporters outside. They rushed to ask if he knew anything about an "imminent announcement" but he just shook his head. Inside, the secretaries were all smiling. The ticket-office people had a spring in their step. Even Mrs Bowman was rattling her tea-trolley along the corridor at a fair old lick. "We think we're going to be all right, Luke!" she giggled, pausing.

"Really?" Luke said. "We're going to beat the deadline?"

"No one knows anything for sure. But Benny's been wheeling and dealing all night, and now he's up with the directors. He won't say a word till he's told you players about it, but we think it's got to be good news. Oh, won't it be wonderful, Luke! We're not going to disappear, after all! We *will* go to Wembley." Her face grew sterner. "*And* we'll win the Cup – whatever that horrible Alan Hansen says on television!"

"Umm," smiled Luke, passing on. "Well, let's see." In spite of the great expectations all around, he didn't feel quite so bright and breezy himself.

Almost certainly there was nothing to worry about. In all probability a real-life consortium of businessmen had finally got the dosh together. These things always seemed to happen at the last minute...

But another thought wouldn't stop nagging at the back of his mind. A thought in the shape of a skinny, bespectacled fan of That Other Lot – a kid so rich that he would hardly *notice* if seven million went out of his account. But no – it couldn't be. It wouldn't make sense. What Miss S had suggested to Cool F. What Luke had then passed on to Benny Webb. It *couldn't* be!

The dressing room was fizzing with fresh hope. "Have you heard, Luke?" cried Craig as soon as he pushed back the door. "Benny's found a buyer! We're gonna get a new chairman! It's all gonna be hunky-dory!"

"We don't *know* that yet," Gaffer reminded him, though he too was smiling.

"Yeah, but it's in the bag, innit?" said Narris.

"All those reporters wouldn't be waitin' outside if Benny didn't have something to tell them. Something *tasty*."

"Right!" agreed Carl. "And then who'll be able to stop us winning the Cup?"

"*No one!*" chorused almost everyone else.

"And I'll tell you what," shouted Half-Fat. "When we do win it, and Gaffer goes up to collect it from..." He paused. "Hey, who *is* presenting the Cup this year?"

"Prince Harry – *Doh!*" Dennis and Madman yelled.

"Yeah well, when we get it from Prince Harry and we're gettin' photographed by everyone, let's *not* take the lid off the Cup and put it on our heads? Every winning team in history has done that. Let's be a bit more original, yeah?"

"*Original?*" laughed Ruel. "But what else can you do with it?"

While all this was going on, Luke quietly got changed. That nagging thought was nagging harder and harder. And when he looked over at Frederick, he could see that the Cool One was uneasy too. As their eyes met, they both asked each other the same awful, silent question: Surely Benny *can't* have?

Then at last the door opened. In strode Benny – followed so closely by Neil Veal that when the Boss abruptly stopped and swung round, Veal cannoned into him and almost lost his footing.

"You," Benny said simply. "Out! This is team business. Now leg it!"

"Was it about Wash and Go?" Chrissie called hopefully as Veal backed out. In reply NV just held up his thumb and first finger, maybe a couple of millimetres closer than before. Then Benny shut the door on him and turned to his team.

"Right then," he began. "You'll all be pleased to know that as of seven-thirty this morning, Albion is no longer a club in crisis. This Castle is not – I repeat *not* – Collapsing. After a night of full and frank discussions with a phenomenally rich man who is, first and foremost, a football fan, a rescue package is now in place. The slate's been wiped clean. All our debts are paid. And that's just the start of it. A whole lot more cash is gonna be injected into this club. We're even gonna get a new purpose-built all-seater stadium up by the motorway. We're on our way, lads. The sleeping giant awakes!"

Luke and Frederick watched in awe as pandemonium broke out. Yes, the team had mobbed Benny after his goal against Exeter, but that was a brisk slap on the back compared to what they did now. After jumping on top of him, picking him up, twirling him round then holding him upside down, they were about to hurl him into the bath when he roared to make himself heard above their racket.

"*There's more!*" he bawled.

So they put him back on his feet and eagerly waited for him to go on.

"As I was about to tell you," he said, after taking a breath, "we have a brand new chairman. We got him into the ground early this morning before the reporters arrived, and even as we speak he's waiting – just through there – to meet you all." He pointed at the bath area. "But not only do we have a new chairman. As part of the deal we have a new *player* as well! Are you ready?"

Luke looked dumbstruck at Frederick. Frederick looked dumbstruck back. Then from behind the bath-area wall walked someone who wasn't exactly a stranger.

"*He's a Winner. He's a Star!*" chanted everyone in the room except Frederick and Luke. "*He's a Prince – a Prince Among Men!*" For it was, of course, none other than James Prince.

"Thanks," JP said with a determined look. Already he was wearing an Albion shirt, over tracksuit bottoms. "I won't make any speeches. I just want to get to work. It's true That Other Lot were my first love. But now that's all in the past. We're going to take this club all the way to the top. Starting right now!"

Luke and Frederick watched everyone cheer and clap. No one noticed that the boys weren't joining in. But only the boys were ready for what came next.

"OK," grinned Madman when the fuss died down. "So where's this new player? It must be someone a bit special with all *your* dosh, Mr Prince!"

"Zinedine Zidane?" guessed Carl. "Juninho? Denilson?"

"Or someone home-grown?" asked Dennis. "Shearer? Campbell? *Owen?*"

There was a brief lull in the proceedings. Benny cleared his throat. Luke shut his eyes. This was it. There was no going back now. The long and winding tale of Castle Albion FC was about to take its most amazing turn of all.

"You're looking at him," Benny announced. "Our new chairman is also our new player."

"And I'm keenly looking forward to making my debut at Wembley!" added JP.

19

No one dared say a word till they were all outside on the pitch. No one could have said a word anyway. "Gobsmacked" didn't *begin* to describe the players' reaction. Then they watched as Princey skidded over, twice, just helping Benny to set up some cones for dribbling around.

"This is a wind-up, right?" muttered Carl.

"It's got to be," Half-Fat hissed back. "And not a very funny one, either."

"I think I'd rather we went bust than have to play with *'im*," grunted Narris.

Luke and Cool F just stood shaking their heads. They knew this was no joke. They knew because Miss S had first put the idea to Frederick, then he had put it to Luke, and Luke in turn had passed it on to Benny: *Tell him that if he buys the club – he can play!* And now incredibly, impossibly, unthinkably, it had happened.

During the warm-up exercises, it became clear that JP wasn't only rubbish at football – he was also staggeringly unfit. While everyone else lapped the pitch ten times – sprinting, jogging, sprinting, jogging – Prince conked out after the first circuit, collapsed over the low perimeter wall and was quite possibly sick on the Town End terrace. He returned to have a go at dribbling round the cones, but five times running he was so comprehensively outwitted by Cone Number One that he simply asked Terry to take it away. Then Cone Number Two managed to get its own back by bashing into JP and leaving him flat on his face.

All the while Benny wouldn't aim one word of criticism at the new boy. Everyone else got as much stick as usual from him, but not young Princey-Wincey. Several times Luke tried to catch the Boss's eye. He wanted to glimpse what the big man was *really* thinking under all the bluster about cash injections and all-seater stadiums. Maybe he would wink. Or even look up at the heavens in despair. But Benny's eye refused point-blank to be caught.

Matters didn't improve when they moved on to practising set-pieces. Prince took two corners, three free kicks and a penalty. Or at least he tried to. He made contact with the ball just once in all six attempts. And after his wild swing at the penalty he seemed to pull a muscle in his bottom, and Terry had to help him over to the touchline for some expert attention.

"VirtuAlarming," remarked Half-Fat, staring across at the Nightmarish Nerd.

"VirtuAltogether*Useless*," Craig agreed.

Then Benny blew his whistle and, with Terry, picked two teams for a practice match. Benny went first and – surprise, surprise – picked JP. As the teams then trotted off to either end, Luke at last got Benny's attention.

"I can't believe you've done this, Boss," he said softly. "I mean, it's brilliant to have saved the club and everything. But *him* – in the *team*! It'll be like playing with ten men from the first minute."

Briefly Benny frowned. "Well, you know how it is in football. More often than not, ten men play out of their skins against eleven and still get a result."

"But it'll be *worse* than having ten men. He'll keep getting in the *way*..."

Benny raised a hand to silence him. "I've taken a calculated gamble, Luke. It was do this or do nothin' and watch Albion go under. So for me there was only ever one option. I think that, in time, you'll *all* find that the advantages will outweigh the – er – disadvantages."

"But Wembley, Boss!" Luke couldn't help going on. "The Cup Final! Who will you leave out on Saturday? How *can* you let him play?"

Benny's answer, as he looked past Luke to

watch JP limp back on to the pitch, was short and sweet: "I can't."

"Sorry?"

"I *can't* let him play. Or more to the point, the FA won't let him. Nothin' was said about the Cup Final during our negotiations. I'm sorry if Mr Prince is under any false impression on that score." Then he looked back at Luke and a flicker of a smile passed across his face.

"I don't understand."

Benny stroked his beard firmly, as if to stop his smile from starting up again. Meanwhile several of the other players had drifted over to listen in. "The transfer deadline for new players was weeks ago. We couldn't 'ave Princey in the side at Wembley even if we wanted to. All we agreed was that he could play in up to twenty games a season." He leaned closer. "That'll kick in as of *next* season. And between you and me, he's such a busy bloke, I can't see him *ever* having the time to turn out for us. Like I said: it's a calculated gamble."

Luke blew out his cheeks. The other players heaved sighs of relief and jogged away to spread the word. "But he *thinks* he's going to play at Wembley," Luke reminded Benny. "What'll he say when he finds out?"

Benny winked. "I've got that in hand. I just need to pick my moment to break it to 'im – and to outline my Plan B. Now then, let's get on with this game!"

He jogged backwards, blew his whistle and watched battle commence.

It wasn't easy – for either side – to play a full-pelt practice match with a kid in glasses wandering about the pitch and occasionally falling over. Cool F played him a few soft balls which he utterly failed to control. Then after fifteen minutes, he was forced to make a mercifully early exit.

It happened by accident. Luke played a short pass to Chrissie who rifled in a low cross. Princey was smack in the way. He seemed to duck and jump at the same time, but the ball zoomed straight at his face – and broke the left-side lens in his glasses. He didn't have another pair with him, so off he had to go.

Benny saw his moment. Tossing his whistle to Terry, he ran across to escort JP off the park, draping a great sheepskinned arm across his narrow shoulders. Soon they were deep in conversation by the dug-out. There was only one thing they could have been talking about. Wembley – and the James Prince No-Show.

Over on the other side of the pitch Luke prayed, very hard, that the new player-chairman would like the sound of Benny's Plan B.

20

In the next two days there were no more calls from Mr Mallard. Luke knew that no news was good news. Whatever Benny had told JP, it must have done the trick.

Meanwhile by rummaging through the swing-bin, Luke was able to check that it *hadn't* all been just a dream. The backpage headlines from the *Daily Mail* left him in no doubt. COMPUTER KID LIFTS CASTLE SIEGE on Thursday. GUNG-HO ALBION CHIEF GOES FOR EURO-GLORY on Friday. (In a press statement, Princey had said he fully expected Albion to win the FA Cup and then "go all the way" in the UEFA Cup next season too.)

After breakfast on Friday, Luke got his week-end bag together and went to wait by the front door for Rodney to drop him off at school. Once he was out of the house, he would be home free. As far as his mum was concerned, he was then going to be in the Peak District until Sunday afternoon.

In fact – as Cool F had told him at school – he would be spending that night with the rest of C Albion Squad at a plush Thames Valley hotel. And then, if everything went to plan at Wembley, he and his team-mates would be ducking Benny Webb in the Trafalgar Square fountains for most of the night after.

"So you've packed everything?" his mum called from the kitchen. "What'll you be *doing* up there anyway? Climbing, walking, visiting places of interest?"

"All of that, really," Luke replied, fingers crossed behind his back. "I think we're going to see a historic building. And maybe a bit of Manchester too."

"Well if you go to a stately home, make sure you bring me a guidebook. And postcards of the gardens. *And* souvenir tea towels, if they've got any."

"Will do." Then Rodney appeared, jangling his car-keys. "See you then, Mum." And he was away. But it wasn't a very high-spirited ride to school. The Pink Pinny Business was *still* playing on Rodney's mind. He really thought Albion had no chance of winning the next day unless he was wearing it at Wembley.

"I went back to the Oxfam shop yesterday," he moaned as they pulled up outside school. "I think I've got a lead on the woman they sold it to. I'll try and track her down today." He stuck out his weak chin. "I've *got* to get it back!"

Luke could only shake his head in wonder. "Relax," he said, touching Rodney's puffer jacket cuff. "We'll do it – pinny or no pinny."

Rodney turned two woeful eyes on his stepson. "If only I could share your confidence," he smiled. Then he wished Luke all the best and clattered off. But at least he was sure of getting to the once-in-a-lifetime game. Mr Mallard had given him a ticket near the Albion bench, and he'd told Luke's mum that he had to be at a regional sales conference in west London. Rodney would be there.

To Luke's surprise, Terry V was waiting by the school gates, almost unrecognizable in a new charcoal suit and club-tie. "Old Rod looks a bit down in the mouth," the player-physio said. "What's 'is problem?"

"He's lost his lucky pink pinny," Luke explained. "You know – the one he wears for all the Cup games? He reckons we can't win without it. And he's gone on about it so much, he's starting to get *me* worried about it now."

"Ah, never mind pink pinnies." Terry took Luke's elbow and began to guide him up to where his blue Metro was parked. "Charcoal suits – *that's* the thing. I'm takin' you over to the ground now to get you measured up. We've all got ours already. We gotta look the part when

117

we go out and inspect the pitch tomorrow, right? Princey's payin' of course. Costs a bomb!"

"But ... but I'm meant to be at school," Luke said.

"All sorted. The head's given you the day off. She says your mind wouldn't be on your work today anyway. Oh, and she says – what were her exact words? – oh yeah: *'Stuff That Red Scum!'* Come on. We'll do some light trainin' too."

When they got to Ash Acre, the place looked as if it *was* under siege. A sea of cameras, boom-mikes and men with stubby pencils were washing up against the walls of the old stadium. Giant-killing Albion had been pretty big news before. Now with JP in the hot seat they were *massive*. But Terry guided Luke through in no time, then took him to an outer office where Princey's personal tailors were waiting to take the Studless Sensation's vital statistics.

Afterwards he changed and went out on to the pitch to knock some balls around with Gaffer, Narris and Carl. At the far end, most of the other players were putting Madman through his paces in goal. But over by the dug-out Benny was having a long chinwag with Chrissie. The kid looked droopy, unusually quiet – not up for it at all. And he'd bundled all his hair into a vast blue-and-white bobble-hat that made him look like the Eighth Dwarf. *Hairy*, perhaps?

"I can't make that lad out," Benny muttered when he came over to Luke's group. "You'd think he'd be walkin' on air on the eve of the Cup Final. I dunno *what's* up with him."

Luke shrugged. "It's probably to do with Wash and Go," he said. "He's been wanting Veal to get him a TV advert for ages. It's really cheesed him off."

"Well let's do something about that," said a young voice behind them. They swung around to find James Prince – all togged up in Albion kit again, and whipping out a mobile phone from the pocket in his shorts. "Wash and Go's made by Procter and Gamble. I know people there. Just give me a moment." He tapped out a number and turned away for a lightning-quick conversation. Then, replacing his phone, he raised a skinny arm and called, "Chrissie!"

The Big-Hair Boy came across, bouncing a ball forlornly in front of him.

"Ten o'clock on Monday at Procter and Gamble's London office," JP told him. "Can you be there? They're putting you in a special one-off commercial."

Chrissie's jaw dropped. Maybe he hadn't fully understood.

"You've done it!" Luke grinned. "Procter and Gamble make Wash and Go. Mr Prince has cracked it for you! You're going to be in their TV advert!''

Slowly, with a tortured expression, Chrissie reached up and lifted his bobble-hat just an inch or so above his head. His *head*. Not his hair. There *was* no hair. No massive trademark mane at all. Just a skull shaved so clean that a baby's bottom looked bearded by comparison! ''I had a Number One,'' he explained in a broken voice. ''I was so sick of waiting on Veal, I got rid of the lot in protest.''

But then as he plonked the hat back on his dome, there was a commotion around the tunnel. Neil Veal surged into view looking *well* pleased. ''Chrissie!'' he cried. ''Wash and Go are history. I've got a bite from Head and Shoulders!''

As the man in Raybans then came dashing towards him, Chrissie began to bounce the practice ball again, eyeing Vealy up and taking careful aim. And when he was no more then five steps away, the Bald One hit it dead ahead on the half-volley. Very hard.

And very, *very* accurately.

21

"We're On Our Way To Wem-bley!
We're On Our Way To Wem-bley!
La-la La Laa! La-la La Laa!"

And for once in the history of Lower-Division-football-chanting, this was true! As the five-star coach wound its way through the sun-soaked suburbs of west London, and C Albion Squad tried to raise its glass roof with their noise, Luke couldn't stop grinning. Or looking at his watch. In just under an hour he would be meeting a member of the royal family. In just *over* an hour he would be taking part in the Showpiece Game of the Season – televised live to so many different countries that half the world would seem to be watching!

It was odd going to a football match in a suit. But the jacket's material was so soft, and the trousers' cut so good, that he hardly noticed he had them on. Every now and then he looked up to see the TV helicopter filming their progress towards the twin towers. And every time he looked out into the streets, more and more people were walking along and waving. It was as if all England was on its way to Wembley – and wearing at least as much blue as red.

"Could I have your attention for a moment, please?" said a voice over the intercom. Luke looked up with the rest to see James Prince on the mike.

"No speeches again," he went on, "but I thought I'd take this chance to wish you luck. I won't cramp your style when we get to the stadium, and besides I'll have other – er – commitments there." He glanced at Benny, who nodded firmly back. "I'm sorry I can't make the team today. But I'm sure you'll all do Albion proud. Enjoy your day. Go for it. I really think you're going to do it."

"*One Mr Prince!*" everyone on the coach roared in appreciation as he sat down. "*There's Only One Mr Prince! One Mr Pri-i-i-nce! There's Only One Mr Pri-ince!*"

Then up he got again, smiling and blushing in his Albion tracksuit. (Why was *he* wearing a tracksuit? Luke suddenly wondered. And what *had* Benny suggested as his Plan B, to keep JP sweet?) "Oh, please," said the Lad With The Loot, "call me what my parents have always called me."

"What's that then, Mr P?" laughed Terry from the back. "*Sir? Your Majesty?*"

"No," he told them. "It's Jimbo." So from that moment on, Jimbo he was.

The last part of the journey – up a jampacked Wembley Way – was unforgettable. Luke felt like a member of the royal family himself, waving at all the punters (and getting some disloyal signals back from That Other Lot's less romantic supporters). Year after year, while his mum was out of the room, he had snatched glances at team coaches arriving like this on TV. Now he was on one himself!

And then he was off it. With almost military efficiency, the team was shepherded inside the Mecca of English Football, then straight through on to the pitch. The players were meant to inspect the hallowed turf, but Luke couldn't keep his eyes down. On TV you never got this sense of a boiling cauldron of sound and colour. And there was *so much* blue and white! "I didn't know we had so many fans!" Luke gasped.

"Yeah right," chuckled Chrissie who was wandering around next to him. "I wonder where *they* all were when we played at Hartlepool in mid-January?"

"Lads, lads, could I have a quick word?" They turned to find ITV's Gary Newbon with a roving mike. "Nice threads," he said, admiring their suits. "And I hear you've just signed a lucrative new advertising deal, Chrissie?"

A little bit bashfully, Chrissie stroked his hairless head. "That's right. Jimbo – er – Mr Prince has got me a long-term contract with the Egg Marketing Board."

Gary N turned to Luke. "Anyone you want to say hello to? Your mum p'raps?"

For a moment, millions of TV viewers saw Luke appear to swallow his tongue. "No, she's not watching," he said finally. "And my dad's here in the stadium. Somewhere. And my stepdad. But there's my grandparents up in Doncaster. Hello Nan and Grandpa!"

"Thrilling times for little Castle Albion?" grinned Gary.

"Not so little now," Chrissie grinned back. "We're getting bigger all the time."

Then it was back to the surprisingly small dressing room – and changing into the stylish new version of the Albion strip that Jimbo had ordered for the day. "Where *is* old Jimbo?" Half-Fat asked when everyone was kitted up. "I thought he'd have been with us." He rolled his eyes "He is a squad member, after all!"

"And where's Terry?" asked Dennis. "Not off with the ferrets, is he?"

"I think you ought to look at this," said Benny in his sub's shirt, switching on a wall-mounted TV. Des Lynam's face appeared. Behind him was the Wembley pitch. Suddenly he swung round, a finger to his earpiece. The camera cut away to the head of the tunnel. And out ran Terry V and Jimbo Prince!

"Well, here's an unexpected addition to the pre-match entertainment," said Des. "Albion physio Terry Vaudeville is bringing out new player-chairman James Prince to be introduced to the army of Albion fans. But – hey – they've got a ball with them. Maybe we're going to see a few tricks..."

"Or maybe we're not," groaned Carl. "He's not gonna try and *kick* it, is he?"

But he was. More than once. More than twice. From his starting-point on the centre spot, JP was planning to dribble all the way to the end where the Albion fans were thickest. Luke held his breath. So *this* was Plan B.

It began badly: JP kicked the ball way too far ahead. It got worse. When he caught up, he air-kicked twice before making contact again. So it went on, with Terry alongside, guiding him towards goal, nudging the ball back into his path.

Des Lynam didn't speak. He didn't have to. The images on the screen said it all. The stadium too had gone eerily quiet – apart from the swelling titters of astonishment from the red-and-white hordes. Then a single awesome voice erupted out of the Albion faithful. Luke knew it anywhere. Rocky Mitford!

"We Love You Jimbo! Oh Yes We Do!"
he assured the boy down on the pitch. Then

30,000 throats opened to sing the same – so loudly that the jeers and boos from That Other Lot's lot were completely drowned out.

Just inside the penalty box now, JP looked up, raised one arm, then at Terry's invitation, he struck a shot at goal. It was quite probably the cleanest kick he'd ever taken. The ball even left the ground for a couple of yards. Then it bounced once, twice, three times – before rolling gently into the net.

Benny reached up and switched off the set as the Albion fans' tumult of delight seemed to shake the whole stadium. "There," smiled the Boss Man. "He got to play at Wembley after all. Now *you've* all got a little date with destiny yourselves. And talking about destiny..." He crossed to where the kit bags were piled up and pulled out four white Marks and Spencer's bags, all bulging with pineapples. "Week in, week out, I give you team talks and you don't take a blind bit of notice. So today I'm gonna try something different."

He took out a pineapple.

"Now I can't help noticin'," he went on, "that whoever gets hit by one of *these* things tends to score a goal..."

"Oh no, Boss! No!" gulped Egghead Pick, seeing what was coming. Then everyone else began to whimper and squeal as well.

"I'm not superstitious as a rule," Benny went

on, "but I'm not prepared to leave any stone unturned. Not on a day like today. So: line up along that wall – all of you! Then turn around and bend over. *Now!*"

The last bit of *Abide With Me* rang out around the stadium. Some of the Albion lads in the tunnel sang along with it. The rest just rubbed their bottoms. That Other Lot, who were standing right next to them, couldn't help taking the micky. "Who's been naughty boys, then?" asked one of the Neville brothers.

Half-Fat scowled back. "Is your dad *really* called Neville Neville?" he said.

"Yeah!" he nodded, squaring up. "What about it?"

"Oh, nothing," peacemaker Dennis cut in quickly. "It's just that *his* dad's called Half-Fat Half-Fat."

And then they were all walking. Striding. Heads high. Marching into the most massive wave of sound Luke had ever imagined – from a crowd twice as big as any that he'd ever played in front of. Past Cup Final players often said that the whole day just flashes past – and you hardly realize what's happened until afterwards. For a few minutes now, everything began to swim for Luke too. The noise... The fans... The colours in the brilliant May sunshine...

He didn't remember lining up next to Madman and Cool F along the edge of the square of red carpet. Nor did he remember – till he saw it later on video – the respectful applause for Prince Harry and his minders as they arrived on the pitch. But halfway through the National Anthem, he felt a soft bang on the knee and finally his wits came back to him.

Looking down, he saw the nutty goalie's lucky Gloster Gladiator twirling around on its length of string – because Madman's hand was shaking so much. "It's OK, Madman," Luke said out of the side of his mouth. "With that hanging up in your goal they'll never score." And history was on his side. Only once in the last two rounds had the plane failed to stop a shot from entering the net.

After the Anthem, Prince Harry was introduced to Gaffer, who then took him down the line to meet the rest of the Albion players. The young royal gave everyone a big grin, and stopped for quite a gossip with Narris.

When Frederick's turn came, the Prince looked keener than ever. "This beats going to school, doesn't it?" he joked with the Cool Boy. And as Gaffer began to tell him who Luke was, he interrupted: "I'm quite aware that this is the

Studless Sensation! It's very good to meet you, Studless. I've followed your career with interest. I'm a rather big TAFKAG fan too. In fact," he leaned closer, "although I'm meant to be neutral, my heart *is* with you underdogs today."

Now Terry V, standing on the other side of Madman, pricked up his ears at that. When *his* turn came to meet and greet Prince H, he leaned forward to make a virtual speech in the young lad's ear. Meanwhile he didn't shake hands once, but twice. And the second time Luke was sure he saw a flash – as if Terry had passed the Prince something small, slim and metallic.

Surely the Albion physio wasn't trying to *bribe* the third in line to the throne! And anyway, how could the lad influence the outcome from up in the royal box? Just over a minute later – after Prince Harry had turned to That Other Lot – Luke understood what had really gone on. No one else in the Albion team seemed to notice. Nor did the TV cameras pick it up. But every time the Prince shook an overdog's hand – Beckham, Giggs, Keane, Cole, Yorke – the player would give a little eye-popping start. Some of them even went up on tiptoe.

Awestruck, Luke glanced down the Albion line. Terry met his eye, then slowly he winked. The guy was incredible! He'd slipped the Prince a little buzzer to give each Red Devil a short, sharp electric shock! Welcome to Wembley!

With That Other Lot still looking puzzled and shaky, each team headed off to the end its fans had made their own.

"We Are The Kings Of The Castle!" hollered Rocky, the South Siders and all the other Albion fans who had now come out of the woodwork. Then they pointed at the far end:

"They're The Dirty Rascals!"

Luke swapped a few passes with Cool F and Dennis. The ball was flying *so* sweetly off his trainers, he couldn't wait to get this show on the road. And after another couple of minutes, he didn't have to wait any more. With everyone on the pitch in position, and everyone in the crowd at fever pitch already, the ref got the Final under way!

There's always the danger Albion might freeze on the day, Trevor Brooking had said. Under this blazing hot sun? With their bottoms still burning from Benny's stunningly accurate pineapple shots? NOT LIKELY! Albion took to Wembley's wide open spaces as if they'd been kept in captivity all season and now at last they'd been let off the leash. "*Express* your-selves," Benny was always telling them. And from the very first minute, they all did just that.

To Luke, it felt as if they weren't playing *on* the pitch at all, but floating an inch or so above it. Everything seemed effortless. Gaffer, Dennis,

Craig, Narris and Chrissie pinged first-time balls back and forth like Brazilians. Ruel and Half-Fat powered along without a hint of their recent limps and jitters. Carl made such a monkey of Japp Stam, outjumping him in the air and out-witting him on the deck, that the desperate Dutchman finally upended him once too often and got a yellow card for his pains.

Madman meanwhile hardly had a thing to do for the whole of the first quarter. And since United were posing so few questions to the Albion defence, Cool F was able to glide upfield for some lipsmacking interplay with Luke.

In the twenty-third minute, the two of them brought the crowd to its feet. Frederick nicked the ball off Dwight Yorke's toe just inside the Albion half. Roy Keane slid in at once to try to win it back, but the Cool One played the cutest one-two with Luke to leave RK threatening thin air – then surged on into the Man U half.

Ruel and Carl made a couple of great runs, forcing the Reds to stretch their defence right across the pitch – and opening up a massive new gap ahead of Cool F. *"Shoot! Shoot! Shoot!"* screamed Rocky and Co as the goal came within his range. But David Beckham had scurried back, got goalside of the Cool One, and begun to head him off towards the right of the MU penalty area.

It looked for a moment as if the danger was passing. But anyone who'd seen Albion equalize against Chester City three weeks before knew better. With Beckham pushing him further wide, Frederick didn't even look behind before back-heeling the ball so gently that it came to a dead stop at the edge of the box.

He'd known that Luke would keep running after the one-two around Keane. And sure enough there was Studless, arriving way before Stam could get in a last-ditch tackle. Luke hit it low and hard. Schmeichel reacted fast, springing up to his right. But the ball deflected off the lunging Stam's thigh and spun wildly to the keeper's *left* instead. Watchers all over the world craned their necks to see if it was going to drop, agonizingly slowly, just inside or outside the post.

The guy with the best view of all – Luke Green – began to raise both arms. Then he had to let them fall. For the ball spun *against* the foot of the post, and rolled across the goal-line into the arms of the grateful, already yelling, Schmeichel.

United were off the hook. They'd got out of jail. Suddenly their fans took fresh heart.

"Uni-TED! Uni-TED! Uni-TED!"
filled the Wembley cauldron for the first time that afternoon. Schmeichel hurled the ball out to Butt and the Reds began at last to take the game to Albion. And Luke, chasing back, had a horrible feeling that millions of people had just witnessed a turning-point.

23

With United's midfield now directing all the traffic, they pressed Albion deep into their own half, and finally gave Andy Cole some decent service.

Taking one Beckham through-ball in his stride, Coley swept past Gaffer and lashed a venomous drive at Madman's Gloster Gladiator. Luckily the keeper was positioned directly in front of it. He stood up well, parried the shot, then fisted it clear when Yorke tried to pounce on the rebound.

Minutes later Ryan Giggs, who was hitting a rich vein of form on the left, crossed at full speed to the far post. Anti-aircraft-gunner Cole got in front of Dennis, hurled himself into the air and met the dipping ball with a spectacular horizontal volley. Again Madman rose to the occasion, though – making himself just big enough to bundle it away.

But the red part of the crowd was smelling blood now. Up at Jimbo Prince's mansion Luke had trembled at those huge VAT sound-blasts. But what he was hearing now – what he was *feeling* in his bones as the animal din grew louder – was no computer-generated Virtu-Racket. This was no cyber-support. For the first time in his brief and brilliant football career, Luke began to feel dwarfed.

There's always the danger they might freeze on the day... Even as Luke raced around chasing the Red Devils' shadows, an icy feeling seemed to numb his stomach. Then his chest and shoulders and even the tops of his legs went cold too. Oh no, oh no, oh no, he thought as he dived in too late for a fifty-fifty ball with Giggs. *Oh no*, he thought, just a minute afterwards, when Keane jumped so far above him to flick a header on to Yorke that he seemed to be flying.

The Reds had their tails up now and no mistake. But as the game came to the boil all around him, red wasn't the main colour on Luke's mind. Crazily, quite crazily, he was thinking *pink*. Pinny pink. What if – after all – Rodney had been right? What if Albion *did* need him to be wearing that thing to go all the way?

He never got a chance to answer his own question. Not then. Cool F saw to that. "Luke! *Luke!*" he bawled to wake up his mate from his fleeting daydream.

Luke was just inside his own half, wide on the

right. When he looked, he saw Frederick speeding out of the Albion defence with the ball – and as he blazed down the central channel, five Man U defenders were trying to read his mind. Luke was the furthest Albion player forward – and he hared off down the touchline expecting Cool F to slide the ball inside the full-back to him. But that was exactly what the Red defence expected too. And the Cool One wrong-footed them all by launching a long pass to the *left*, where Chrissie was making the run of his life.

The stadium seemed to quake. The Boy With No Hair reached the ball ten yards from the byline. Every other Man U player was behind him, so Peter Schmeichel had to dash out to force him wider. Chrissie, however, saw him coming. And as the Great Dane slid across, he looped the most exquisite little cross back over Schmeichel's blond head.

It was as if Cool F had taken Alan Hansen's white pen and marked the precise spot where he wanted the ball returned. Berg did his level best to keep up with the Albion dude as he hurtled towards the unguarded goal, but it was no contest. Frederick met Chrissie's cross on his chest, let the ball drop to his right knee, then before it hit the ground he swept it right-footed into the roof of the net.

The stadium *did* quake then. Albion were in

front! And Luke was the first to rush across and leap on the scorer. Chrissie, the provider, wheeled away with his shirt-front pulled up over his face to reveal the home-scrawled T-shirt message underneath: *I Have Seen The Future*... But in his excitement he forgot to pull up the back to show the rest of it. Prince Harry punched the air in the royal box, and from Rocky and the South Siders came an ear-splitting:

"You're Cool! And You Know You Are! You're COOL...!"

Benny was up off the Albion bench though – windmilling away, miming at his lads to "Focus! Focus! And *Stay* Focused!" But there was no danger of them losing concentration now. With Luke right back on song, they tore into Man U. And just on the stroke of half-time Carl went staggeringly close to doubling their lead with a header past the post from one Studless corner.

Albion's fans gave the Div Three Have-A-Go Heroes a rip-roaring ovation as they went off. Benny too was all smiles in the dressing room. "Good half, son," he said as each player came in, parked himself down and glugged back his tea.

"There'll be a few cups flying in next door!" Gaffer joked.

"Yeah," said Terry. "I was watchin' old Fergie

after the goal went in. He was chewin' so hard on his gum, I thought he was gonna bite right through his cheek and start gnawin' on the bloke next to him!" Then he nudged Luke. "Not worried about that old pinny of Rod's *now* then?"

"You've been a credit to the game, lads," nodded Benny. "All I ask is that you go out there and bang in Goal Number Two. That'll kill 'em off for good! You'll see – that second goal will be the most important!"

"Oh, but young Fred's here wasn't exactly *trivial*, was it?" cried Dennis, hugging the kid who still looked as cool as a mountain stream while everyone around him was sweating buckets.

"Too right," Terry V agreed. "And d'you know who was goin' more ape than anyone else around our way when you scored? Jimbo's PA – Miss Sanchez. I reckon you've scored there too, son." He winked and everyone wolf-whistled.

"OK, OK," Benny shouted as the interval ended. "There'll be plenty of time for all that *after* the game. Now keep your eyes on the ball, you lot. In an hour's time I wanna be getting my hands on that beautiful big Cup."

"No sweat, Boss," grinned Craig on his way out. "Only *don't* put the lid on your head, will you? Half-Fat's orders!"

24

Albion began the second half just as they'd started the first. Confidence oozed from all eleven players as they defended their lead with amazing poise – and even found time to catch Man U on the occasional break. If they'd ever expressed themselves more eloquently on a pitch, Luke didn't remember it.

As for the Reds, they looked as if they'd had another dose of electric-shock treatment in the dressing room – this time from Alex Ferguson and a cattle-prod. They buzzed about the field like men possessed – expressing *them*selves too, although mostly in words of four letters which were mainly aimed at each other. Luke took note. It was always a good sign when opposition players fell out. Meanwhile the massed Red ranks were making precious little noise.

The same could not be said about Albion's thousands. Did they *sing*! If by some chance Man U managed to score and force the game into extra time – surely South Side Rocky and the rest would be too hoarse to chant another word. When they weren't telling Albion how much they loved them, or standing up to show how much they hated That Other Lot, they kept on pointing at the BBC gantry and chorusing:

"Five-Nil? Five-Nil? Five-Nil?"

and:

"Hansen, Hansen, Take Off Your Pants!"

Luke couldn't help smiling every time he heard that. And the way he stroked the ball around put a smile on his team-mates' faces too. Quite simply he was passing Beckham, Butt and Giggsy off the pitch. And Roy Keane couldn't do a thing to shut him down. Nothing legal, at any rate.

Then in the seventy-third minute, Luke nutmegged him in the centre-circle. Keane threw caution to the wind and Studless to the ground. It was, as Barry Davies would have said, "a very untidy challenge". But the ref made a very tidy note of Keaney's name before brandishing a yellow card in his face. The look Roy then gave Luke showed that he'd *definitely* crossed him off his Christmas card list.

After that Luke got the underdogs' tails wagging again with a series of special passes into the paths of Chrissie, Carl and Ruel. Twice Schmeichel had to storm out of his area to reach the ball before the Albion men – all his defenders were now playing as extra midfielders in the rabid Red quest for an equalizer. Finally Big Peter must have felt left out. Because when a wayward Giggs cross hit Gaffer's shin and bounced behind for a corner, *he* ran upfield as well.

He'd done this sort of thing before, of course. It unsettles a defending team when the other goalie pops up in its own six-yard box. Schmeicho had even snatched a late goal in a European tie at Old Trafford. But that was completely freakish. It couldn't happen twice. Not with the same player. *Could* it?

There was a lot of argy-bargy as David Beckham ran over to take the corner. Ruel, who had been marking Stam, now stuck like a limpet to Schmeichel's side, leaving Carl to watch the Dutchman. So many bodies were crammed into such a tight space that suddenly, amid all the jockeying and jostling, all four guys stumbled over the line and *into* the goal, where they promptly fell over.

It looked harmless enough. None of it seemed pre-planned. Back on the penalty spot, Roy Keane blazed at the ref that the MU men had been pushed but no one took any notice. Then as Schmeichel struggled back to his feet, he put out a big gloved hand to grab the back stanchion. In doing so he somehow loosened the string that Madman had used to hang his Gloster Gladiator.

Did Schmeich do it on purpose? Was it a total

accident? A million TV replays later, it was still impossible to be sure. But however it came about, everyone saw what happened next. The plane plummeted groundwards – but Madman dived full-length to catch it just inches from the turf. To a gigantic "*Olé!*" from the crowd, he staggered to his feet with a grin. And he was about to start retying the knot when the ref blew for the corner to be taken.

Madman, both hands full, glanced at him in panic. The ref just waved play on. There was, after all, nothing in the rules about taking time out to re-fasten a lucky charm. And Beckham had already begun his run-up. All the crazy keeper could do was lob the plane gently into the back of the net and get himself into position. Which was exactly what he did.

But as he turned to face the high, inswinging ball he heard a dreadful snap as the plane hit the deck. He couldn't resist looking back to find one beloved wing broken in two. And when he twisted back round, too late now, the ball sailed right over his head and right *on to* the head of Mr Ryan Giggs.

Giggsy made no mistake from one yard out. His header bulged the back of the net. Then to add insult to injury, the ball dropped on to the Gladiator's tailplane and broke that off too. One-one! And one lucky charm now missing in action.

The next minute or so was nightmarish. As

Luke tried to console the desperate Madman the crowd began its own bombardment.

"Uni-TED! Uni-TED!! Uni-TED!"

seemed to be vibrating every hair on Luke's body. The Reds' fans were jumping around so much that a whole section of the stadium seemed to be dissolving before his eyes. *The second goal will be the most important*, Benny had predicted. And as Ruel kicked off again to Carl, who immediately gave it away to Cole, Luke was terrified he'd been right.

Cole waltzed round Half-Fat, played a one-two with Yorke, took the return just outside the box and fired in a wickedly-swerving shot that beat Madman all ends up. Luckily it beat the far post too and spun away to safety. Yet Albion couldn't stem the Red tide. Straight from the goal kick, Beckham tried one of his long-range efforts – firing a vicious fifty-yard lob back in. Again Madman was nowhere. This time the ball bounced on top of his bar and over.

All Albion's dreams had crashed with Madman's plane. *With that hanging up in your goal they'll never score*, Luke had said so cockily before the game. But what about when it *wasn't* hanging up? Why had he dared to tempt fate like that? Fate, fate, fate, fate, *FATE*! Rodney hadn't been wrong. The writing had been on that blessed pink pinny all along. That missing pink pinny. FATE!

Little teams like Albion weren't *meant* to tonk the likes of Man U at Wembley. It just wasn't in God's script. "And on the sixth day, after an early scare, He watched the Premier League giants have the Div Three minnows for dinner." *That*'s what destiny was all about. Pineapples didn't come into it!

Benny was signalling like fury on the line. Two minutes to go. Albion *had* to try to hold out for extra time. Another half an hour... Anything could happen... But Luke looked around him, and he knew that it wasn't true.

Albion's zing had gone. Craig, Dennis, Narris and Half-Fat – all so sprightly before – now looked as if they were wading through a vat of Vaseline. Gaffer, Carl and Ruel had their socks rolled down, and every step seemed to drain more out of them. Even Chrissie's hairless head had dropped. And Madman – well, the guy now seemed to be in tears when he wasn't watching shots from Giggs, Beckham, Butt and Yorke whistle past his posts.

Luke felt like crying himself as he twisted round to give chase as Gaffer managed to head a Keane cross away. Stam smoothly killed the ball on his chest, and waved his fellow-defenders forward yet again. The Reds weren't interested in an extra half-hour. The game was theirs for the taking right away.

Carl should have closed Stam down but his

legs wouldn't take him there. So the big stopper dribbled on into Albion's half. Luke was the nearest player now.

"Shut him! Shut him! Shut him!" Cool F called from the back. Yet Luke's own legs seemed about to buckle. Out of the corner of his eye he saw Benny holding up one finger. One minute to go.

But just behind the Boss he glimpsed something else. Something bobbing madly about. Something ... *pink*!

Luke couldn't believe it. Rodney! In the pinny! There by the Albion bench! He must have gone to that woman's house and managed to get it back! So if this really *was* all about Fate, then did this mean that Albion still had a chance?

"Shut him down, Luke," Frederick yelled again. "Shut him or we're dead."

Like a ferret in a dressing room, Luke launched himself forward. Seeing him come, Stam paused to measure up a pass to Keane who'd run out wide on the right. Big Japp nudged the ball sideways one last time and aimed to let fly. His boot never touched it again. Someone else got there first. Someone Studless.

Luke slid in from at least five yards away – and toe-poked the ball past Stam. As the startled stopper turned to get it back, Luke sprang up and skipped around his other side.

There was never any doubt who would win *this* race. Stam knew it too. Sliding in himself, he tried to hack Luke down. But Luke guessed what was coming – and started his jump a split-second earlier.

Stam flew beneath him and out of the picture. Luke landed again, the ball at his feet, and looked up to see *no one* between him and Schmeichel in the Manchester goal! Off he set. But so did Schmeichel. From up in the pricey seats it must have looked amazing. The biggest bloke on the pitch making a beeline for the smallest – and apparently intent on smashing him to a pulp.

There were no two ways about it: Schmeichel had opted for one hundred per cent intimidation. He didn't stop at the edge of his box but kept up the charge – his arms spread wide, and his mouth – it seemed – even wider.

The goal looked like a speck behind him. Luke felt like a speck in front of him. But there was one little thing he had that Big Bad Pete didn't have. The ball. You can be as big as you like. You can make as much noise as you like. But at the end of the day this most brilliant, most simple of games is all about a ball.

And Luke didn't want the ball any more. He'd had enough running and kicking. But he knew exactly how to get rid of it. He knew *just* the right place for it.

With Schmeichel only five giant steps away

from him, he stroked the leather sphere with the outside of his right foot. There wasn't much pace on it. Not much accuracy either – as far as everyone watching could see. Luke seemed to have aimed for the left-side corner flag. As it soared past Schmeichel, the stranded keeper hardly even made an attempt to reach for it. Safe, he thought.

But once it was past him its path changed. It began to veer inwards. Sharply. *Very* sharply. Then as it got nearer the goal, and lost height, it completed an arc that was more or less the same shape as one of the twin towers up above.

Oh, and it crossed the goal-line after one bounce and snuggled itself into the back of the net.

All about a ball.

To coin a football phrase: Luke had scored a goal.

"Yeeeaaaahhhhhhhh!"

By the time the crowd erupted, Luke was already flying towards the touchline. Benny Webb was on his feet waiting – arms stretched out even wider than Schmeichel's. Luke leapt up and wrapped his arms and legs around the sheepskin. "*Yess! Yesss! Yesssss! YESSSSS!*" went Benny.

Then as everyone else came zooming over – tired legs? *What* tired legs? – Luke jumped down, turned, and had his head grabbed then kissed by Terry. Or *was* it Terry? As Luke wiped the slobber off his forehead, all he could see was a blur of pink. *Rodney?* No, it was Terry all right – but wearing a pink pinny over his track-suit! *That*'s what Luke had seen. *That*'s what had lifted his spirits!

"I thought I'd stick it on just in case you got worried!" Tel yelled in explanation, plucking at the frilly vile-coloured fabric. "It's all in the flippin' mind anyway, innit? Oh you *beauty*!" And he gave Luke another smacker.

Then the scorer vanished under a blue-and-white hooped avalanche. Luke might never have come out if the ref hadn't personally pulled half the players off. He wasn't having any nonsense. Pointing at his watch, he ordered them all back to their berths on the pitch. It wasn't quite over. The guy on the line had already shown the crowd that there was one minute of Time To Be Added On.

One minute. But as Brian Clough once said, it only takes a second to score a goal. And straight from the kick-off, all eleven Man U players stormed into the Albion half desperate to do just that. Schmeichel even took off his gloves. He had no plans to use his hands again until United were level.

Yorke played it out to Beckham, who skipped past Half-Fat and slipped it inside to Keane. He looked up, saw Cole darting into the box behind Gaffer and chipped up a perfectly-weighted pass for him to run on to.

But Gaffer read the ball's flight well. Taking three steps back, he jumped high and just got his head to it. As it came down, he caught it on his right instep.

"Welly it! Welly it! Welly it!
Anywhere Will Do!"

pleaded tens of thousands of blue-and-whites. And wellying it anywhere was – to be quite honest – what Gaffer usually did best. Over the North Stand at Ash Acre. Or high above the

South Side. But this was Wembley – and here, today, he dreamed up a different way to kill off Man U's challenge once and for all.

Deftly he flicked up the ball again, then gave it a sky-high blast – not towards the left touchline, not towards the right, but straight down the pitch. No United player made a genuine attempt to chase back. No one would have reached it anyway. Gawping as it sailed above their heads, they let their shoulders drop.

The ball bounced the first time between the centre-circle and Schmeichel's vacant penalty area. It bounced again just before the six-yard box. And when it bounced for a third time, it had just entered the goal. THREE-ONE!

There was no way back for United now. They knew it. Albion knew it. Everyone watching knew it. Even the ref knew it. So he took one last look at his watch, gave three blasts on his whistle, and brought the proceedings to an end.

Suddenly time seemed to rush forward *and* stand still. For a dizzying moment Luke even thought he might faint. All around him Man U players were squatting down, dejected.

"Al-bi-on! Al-bi-on! Al-bi-on!"
pulsed inside his head, as well as from every blue-and-white bit of the ground. It was true. All of this really was true. The impossible had happened. Jack had slain the giant. *Castle Albion had beaten Man United to win the FA Cup!*

Then Luke was half-walking, half-running towards the bench – half under his own steam, half being carried by Narris and Madman. The first face he saw was James Prince's, hair flying, glasses askew, pimples rampant, tears in his eyes. "Fantastic! Brilliant! Fairytale! Magic!" he gasped, hugging Luke like a long-lost cuddly-toy. "Marvellous! Superb! Smashing! Fabulous!"

"Don't hold back!" Narris laughed, kissing him. "Say what you really feel!"

Then Benny Webb scooped Luke up in one arm, Frederick in the other, and hopped along the touchline in a crazy jig that was part victory dance, part child abduction. When he put them down, and nine other players leapt on top of them to squirm about like a pile of jubilant Third Division maggots, all Benny could do was wipe his eyes and stutter: "It's... It's... Oh this is... It's got to be... How can I...? Never in my..."

"Well that's easy for you to say, Boss!" thundered Terry V, still in the decoy pink pinny, before hurling himself at the Big Boss Man and giving him such a squeeze that his sheepskin baaah-ed for mercy. Meanwhile Rodney and TAFKAG were burrowing into the maggots to drag out Luke and Frederick.

"We 'ad 'em! We 'ad 'em! We 'ad the flippin' Man U!" ranted Rod, jumping up and down with Luke's head gripped tightly under his arm. Thankfully TAFKAG wrenched him free and

beamed at his battered boy. "This," he boomed, "is better than The Beatles!" before giving him the father of all bearhugs. Then Gaffer grabbed him, then Dennis, then Craig, then Carl ... then most of the Albion fans in the stadium, for all Luke knew. This was less like a football event now than going the distance with Mike Tyson. And although Luke didn't get his ear chewed off, he *was* almost deafened by a truly earth-shaking chant of:

"We Love You Albion, Oh Yes We Do!"

He had no idea how long it all went on. But it was a major relief to be rescued by the Wembley officials and led across with the rest of the winners to the foot of the thirty-nine steps to the royal box. Man U were already trooping up there, miserably receiving their runners-up medals from Prince H – one or two then turning to give their own fans a sorry wave.

Luke found himself lining up behind Chrissie, who had swapped shirts with Giggsy and was pulling the Red one over his head. Luke just caught a glimpse of the rest of the *I Have Seen The Future*... message on his back: ...*And It's Eg-Shaped!* Chrissie never had been the world's greatest speller.

Then up they were going! Bobbing and weaving to avoid the host of clutching hands, it seemed to take another forty-five minutes to get to the top. But there at last was Gaffer Mann –

scorer of the game's clinching goal, Albion's senior pro who had played his whole career in the League's basement – pumping the hand of Prince Harry, gripping the loveliest trophy in football, then hoisting it aloft to a rapturous reception from Albion's overjoyed faithful.

Luke hadn't even *seen* a bottle of champagne yet, but a million bubbles shot up his nose. And when his turn came to get his medal, the Prince leaned down and said in his ear: "That was quite magnificent, Studless. I'm arranging for you all to come back to the palace later. We'll have a jolly good knees-up. Grandma won't mind at all!" Luke laughed. So he *would* be seeing a stately home!

Cool F was right behind him, and when they got back down to the pitch, they looked – goggle-eyed – at each other's medals, then high-fived.

"Cool," smiled Frederick.

"Smart," replied Luke, nodding at the person who had draped herself around the Cool One from behind to get a closer look at his silverware. Miss Estella S – a higher class of footballer's friend than Posh Spice *any* day of the week.

"Luke! Frederick! Just the guys I want to see!" In a flurry of Boss suit, Raybans and fluttering paperwork, Neil Veal was upon them – closely followed by TAFKAG and Terry V. "*Monster* performance!" he grinned, gold teeth glinting in the mellow Wembley sunshine.

"Absolute *monster*! I've just been tipped the wink about tomorrow too. Castle Rap's gonna be Number One – by a mile! And now they want a TAFKAG and Albion album!" He whipped out a pen and shoved the papers under Luke's nose. "So I've just signed up your dad to represent *him* in all areas – and finally he's OK'd it for *you* to sign along with him."

Luke smiled at chart-topping TAFKAG, who gave him a big thumbs-up. "Well, why not?" said Studless, scribbling one of the two names Vealo most wanted.

"Mega!" he whooped, transferring pen and papers in a flash to Cool F. "You too, Frederick. I'm gonna take you places you never even dreamed of!"

Frederick raised an eyebrow but pulled free of Miss S to sign his name anyway. "Album?" he asked, passing back the contracts. "Ace."

"You won't regret this, boys!" Vealy purred, offering his hand first to Luke. "I'll make you bigger than Owen and Oasis put together!" As Luke shook, he thought he saw Terry slip something to Frederick. When his mate's turn came to press the flesh, he *knew* that Terry had done it. Just like Man U before the kick-off, Agent Veal got an unexpected shock. "*Aaaarrrgggghhhhhh!*" he cried as his Raybans fell off, his eyes crossed, his tan went purple and his hair struggled to stand up through all the gel. But as soon as the Cool One let go, he brought himself back down to earth. "Let's do post-match celebration banquet!" he twinkled.

"Lads, come on!" Benny shouted from just a few yards away. All the Albion players had their medals now and the world's press was begging for a team snapshot. Raggedly they got themselves into a group – singing along deliriously with Rocky's Enormous Chorus of:

"We're On Our Way To Europe!
We're On Our Way To Europe!"

That was true too. The UEFA Cup beckoned. What on earth was Luke going to tell his mum if Albion had to play away in Russia or Malta or Iceland?

It was a pretty weird team group. TAFKAG was in there. Rodney. Jimbo and Miss S. Luke and Cool F knelt down at the front with the cup, while directly behind them was ... Luke had to blink at this: old Mrs Bowman the tea-lady!

"Ooh, I'm so *excited*!" she quivered above her vast blue-and-white scarf. "I haven't had so much fun since we won the war!" Then she lurched forward over Luke's shoulder, snatched the lid off the FA Cup and was about to plonk it on her blue-rinsed head when Half-Fat yelled, "Don't! Don't! *Don't!*"

He could have saved his breath. A passing hand reached out and whipped the lid away. A hand at the end of an arm. A bare arm.

It all happened so fast that Luke didn't realize its owner was *completely* naked until he covered his rudest bit of all with the Cup lid and streaked away across the pitch.

"Han-sen! Han-sen! Han-sen!" bayed the disbelieving crowd. And it *was* him. Old Aggro Alan – a man of his word if ever there was one. And boy, did he *shift*! He could have given Marc Overmars a ten-yard start and still beaten him to the other side. Once there, Trevor Brooking met him with a Union flag, marked *Castle Albion FC*, to cover up his modesty. The number of women fans who fainted was officially given afterwards as two hundred and forty-six.

"All right, you lot," said the nearest photographer as the pack behind him all trained their cameras back on the true heroes of the day, the season, the year, the decade – *any* decade. "Tell us who you are then!"

"*We...*" roared Luke Green, Frederick Dulac, Madman Mort, Benny Webb, Terry Vaudeville, Jimbo Prince, Estella Sanchez, Craig Edwards, Rocky Mitford, Dennis Meldrum, Gaffer Mann, Chrissie Pick, Half-Fat Milkes, Narris Phiz, Carl Davey, Ruel Bibbo, Rodney, TAFKAG and Mrs Bowman the tea-lady, "*... are the Kings of the Castle!*"

And there wasn't a single person – anywhere – who disagreed with them.

Come and have a go at the whole series:

COME AND HAVE A GO IF YOU THINK YOU'RE SMART ENOUGH!

COME AND HAVE A GO IF YOU THINK YOU'RE COOL ENOUGH!

COME AND HAVE A GO IF YOU THINK YOU'RE MAD ENOUGH!

COME AND HAVE A GO IF YOU THINK YOU'RE RICH ENOUGH!